WHY DID YOU
LEAVE ME?

WHY DID YOU LEAVE ME?

JANE CLAYPOOL MINER

SCHOLASTIC BOOK SERVICES

New York Toronto London Auckland Sydney Tokyo

For June and Denzil

ISBN 0-590-30229-9

12 11 10 9 8 7 6 5 4 3 2   0 1 2 3 4 5/8

Printed in the U.S.A.   06

CHAPTER 1

Laura Manning smoothed the heavy cream on the delicate tissue around her eyes. Her fingers worked efficiently as she rubbed cream into the vertical creases between her brows.

Sixteen and wrinkled, Laura thought. *Thanks, Mama.* She could almost hear her mother saying, "Eggshell skin, Laurie. It's like porcelain, so take care of it."

Her mother's skin had had that same pink-white clearness that flushed with the wind, burned in the sun, and crackled with age if you weren't careful. Her mother had been a beautiful woman until she was thirty-two. That year, her skin had dried up and died before it bloated.

Laura frowned at her reflection. *Do I look like her?* The familiar feeling started in her stomach. Having a drunk for a mother made you worry a lot — even after she left town.

Laura stuck her tongue out at her own reflection. She answered herself aloud, "Of course you look like her. Who else? Thin-skin and bad blood tell. Born to sin and what's more, you're late." The clock said a quarter to six.

She didn't want Don to have to wait for her. It made her feel funny to have people wait for her. Well, it wasn't exactly a funny feeling, that was the trouble. *Nothing funny about an ulcer*, Laura thought as she pulled on her jogging suit and started down the stairs.

She paused in the kitchen long enough to drink a glass of milk and write her brother Tommy a note. She pinched a couple of leaves off the geraniums in the window sill and stared out at the dawn. *Mama, Mama, how are you? Where are you? Why don't you write anymore? Are you dead? Why did you die, Mama? Why did you go off and leave me to take care of Tommy and Dad?*

Laura shook her head briskly, as though she could exorcise the thoughts, and went out the door. The cold air caught her by surprise and she took a deep breath, then started jogging down her driveway and out onto the street.

She was past the library before she remembered her dream. It had been in technicolor and Don was in it with his red hair as bright as day. Don had been wearing a green jogging suit and he was listening very seriously as Laura explained the situation to him. It was a perfectly ordinary dream, except Laura hadn't been Laura at all. She'd been the White Rabbit from *Alice in Wonderland*.

Laura smiled at the memory of the White Rabbit who was struggling so seriously to explain to Don that she couldn't be his partner on the track team. Now that she was awake, she could see that she resembled that White Rabbit quite a bit. She was always worried about being late and she was frightened most of the time. Anxiety, the doctor called it.

Well, that doctor would be anxious too if he had to think about keeping up his grades, hold on to a social life, and do all the chores around the house. Today, for instance, Laura had to remember to sew the patches on Tommy's cub scout uniform after she finished the cleaning. It would be an ordinary day and if she worked hard, she'd be finished by supper. Then she could get to work on her history project — if she wasn't too tired.

Laura knew she was worrying while she was jogging. What would Dr. Thomas think of that? He'd suggested a half hour of running each morning as a tension relief. He'd said, "I don't want to put you on tranquilizers if I can help it. Try fresh air and exercise first."

As she'd waited for the prescription for the incipient ulcer, the doctor asked, "What do you hear from your mother?"

"Nothing." Laura's face had burned red at the mention of her mother. Her mother had been a great believer in tranquilizers and there had been some bad scenes. Laura could still remember the night before her mother went away. This same doctor had refused to come out.

"Put her in the hospital," he said and slammed the telephone down in Laura's ear. That had been an awful night. Her father hadn't been able to hold her mother back, and she ran into the street screaming about how cruel he was. No one ever spoke of her mother. Why was he asking?

The doctor chuckled. "She was a beautiful girl

too. But you're even more beautiful. For a minute, though, I thought it was Gloria sitting in that chair."

The doctor looked at her shrewdly and asked, "I suppose you worry about being an alcoholic?"

Laura shook her head. She'd already figured that one out. You couldn't be an alcoholic if you didn't drink, and Laura had no intention of ever drinking.

The doctor patted her on the shoulder. "Don't worry, get lots of exercise, and come back and see me in a month or two. We'll get you straightened out fast."

And it was true that the running had helped — or was it only that she'd met Don jogging one morning? Was her stomach better because she had a boyfriend?

Laura turned the corner onto North Street and ran lightly up to Don who was jogging in one place under the lights of the broken YMCA sign. She said, "Sorry I'm late." Then she giggled. She *did* sound like the White Rabbit.

Don smiled and said, "One of us had to be first, Laurie."

He turned and they started jogging on Main Street, past the three movies, the one department store, the three ten-cent stores, and then to the outskirts of town. They followed Main Street until it turned into Prospect Avenue and bent around the lake. They followed the road for a while, then turned onto a path that circled the lake. There was still ice on the edges of the lake but the footpath was clear enough.

Laura loved this path. On the days when it was

her turn to choose, she often headed for the lake. Since she and Don started running together, they made an agreement to take turns leading the way. That was Don's idea and Laura had been grateful because she knew that she would have run wherever he said and never even thought about her own preferences. Then Don seemed to choose *her* favorite paths when it was his day. *He wants to please me*, Laura thought.

Suddenly, Laura Manning felt good about herself, about Don, about this morning. She looked out over Clearview Lake to the hills on the other side. The ski slopes were closed and it would soon be time for picnics. Did Don like fried chicken? Potato salad?

They turned back onto the road, ready to circle into town. Don's summer project had been to clock every possible run in Pittsfield, and this one was eleven miles. On school days they stuck to the shorter ones, but this was Saturday morning, and when they finished they would go to the Soda Shop for breakfast. It was part of their bargain and today was Laura's turn to buy.

Good to be alive, Laura thought. She seemed to be younger, happier, after these runs, so the doctor was right. Or was it only that Don was running beside her? Would she still be running at all if she were alone?

They passed Marilyn Rogers and her friend Evelyn on the corner of Main and Spring. Marilyn was wearing a pink jogging suit with her black hair tied back with a scarlet scarf. *She's after Don,* Laura thought as the two girls ran past.

Laura wasn't worried about Marilyn. She might

have a pink jogging suit but Don was interested in *her* — Laura. Marilyn would have to run alone or, with someone else. Don was *her* partner. Laura was still feeling great as they came up Main Street and stopped at the door of the Soda Shop.

The Soda Shop opened at six-thirty and they were the first customers of the morning. Laura and Don sat at the only booth which still had the red trim around the edges of the black leather. On their first morning together, Laura had picked it, saying it was the classiest. Now it was *their* booth.

They ordered cocoa, ham and eggs, and bagels and cream cheese, giggling at their appetites. It was a wonderful morning, Laura thought. She was sure Don was going to ask her to go to the movies tonight. If he did, she would say yes and let the history report slide.

Don smiled at her and asked, "You're going to be able to make the track team, aren't you. Laura?"

She sipped her cocoa and felt her stomach tighten into knots. "I explained it to you, Don. I can't."

"I know you have to take care of your brother but the team will practice early in the morning. Tommy's old enough to pour his own cereal."

Laura smiled and shook her head. "Not cold cereal. I don't permit junk foods."

Don leaned forward and put his hand over hers. He said softly, "Laura, I want you for my partner. I want to be on that track team and I want to win. We could go to the Finals."

Laura shook her head. "I can't. I've got responsibilities."

"You sound like an old woman when you say that." Don sounded angry.

Laura wanted to crumple into a ball and hide, or cry out that she was doing the best she could. Instead of those dramatics, she spoke softly. "I do have responsibilities, Don. I don't want Tommy to feel the way I did when I was his age. Do you know what it does to a kid to be abandoned?"

"It isn't the same," Don answered. "Your mother really did abandon you, Laura, because she drank. All I'm asking is that you join a co-ed track team that will practice on Saturday mornings. I'll even help you with the housework in the afternoons if you want."

But Laura could only say stiffly, "You've been talking to people about my mother."

Don shook his head. "I didn't have to talk to anyone about your mother. Everyone knows your mother drank too much and ran off and left you and Tommy. It's all old news, Laurie. It's in the past."

Laura spoke stiffly, "It may be old news to you but it's my life. I don't want to talk about it."

Don shook his head. "Sorry." Then he said, "Look, Laurie, I want to win and I want to win with you. Talk to your father and see what you can do. I'll pick you up at eight. New movie in town — all about this giant spider that eats a warehouse full of records, then broadcasts the hit tunes as he chases mortals."

Laura knew she was supposed to laugh and pretend everything was all right, but she didn't feel like it. She was still bothered because Don seemed to know too much about her family life.

Had he been talking to other people about Gloria? She would hate that. Why couldn't he understand that Tommy deserved the best she could give him?

She tried to think of something else to say so that the knots in her stomach would untie, but all she could think of was running away. She couldn't run from Don, though, because Don was special. A few minutes ago she had thought he was the most special person in the world. Now she was confused because he insisted she do something she was convinced was wrong.

As though he read her thoughts, Don said, "I'm sorry, Laurie. I know you have it tough, but I'm not going to just drop this. See if you can work it out. Then, if you can't, I'll get someone else." He touched her hand lightly and said, "No matter what, you'll be my girl. OK?"

Laura nodded. The knots loosened a bit. That someone else was apt to be Marilyn Rogers because Marilyn was a good runner too. It was nice of Don to tell her that whatever happened with the track team, their relationship wouldn't be affected. Laura almost believed it because she knew Don was steady. Still, if Don and Marilyn became a team . . .

As though on cue, Marilyn Rogers and Evelyn came into the Soda Shop and over to their booth. Evelyn pulled a chair over and plopped down, saying, "I hate jogging! I only do it because Marilyn promised me I'd look just like her in six weeks!"

Everyone laughed. Evelyn was short and plump, but Marilyn was almost six feet tall and very slim. Even Laura, who was five feet seven inches tall and weighed one hundred and twenty pounds, felt fat around Marilyn.

Marilyn looked cool and beautiful as she stood quietly beside Evelyn's chair. When Laura moved over so Marilyn could sit beside her, Marilyn said, "No thanks. We don't want to bother you. I just wanted to tell you I'm looking for a partner for the co-ed track team, so if you hear of anyone, let me know."

Laura tensed as she said, "Don is looking for someone because I don't have time."

Marilyn sounded sincere as she said, "Oh, Laura, what a shame!"

Laura stood up, knocking over a glass of water. She just couldn't bear to sit in that booth another minute. She said, "I have to go. It's nine and Tommy will be worried about me." She was paying the check when Don caught up with her.

He asked, "What's the matter?" When she didn't answer, he asked, "See you tonight. Eight?"

"Sure," she nodded. She wanted to get out of that place before the tears spilled out. She ran all the way home, tears streaming down her cheeks.

She wasn't exactly sure why she was crying, but when she opened the door to the kitchen and found Tommy standing by the sink, spilling a cup of cocoa all over the floor, she had an excuse. "Oh, Tommy!" she wailed.

He dropped the cocoa cup on the floor and held out his hand for inspection, whining. "You're late. I've burnt myself and your note said nine. It's already nine-thirty. Look, I've burnt myself."

Laura couldn't stop looking at the cocoa-covered floor she would have to mop, at the cabinets covered with cocoa that she would have to clean. She burst into tears. "It's not fair!" She sobbed as she bent down and began wiping up the mess.

Tommy whined for a minute. Then he put on his jacket and went outside. Laura was still mopping when her father came into the kitchen and asked, "Crying over spilt milk?"

Laura sobbed louder. As her father helped her to her feet, saying, "Now, now, Cinderella," he was laughing. He asked, "What happened? Tommy turn into a monster from the late-late show?"

She shook her head. "It's not just Tommy. It's Don and Marilyn and . . ." Between sobs, she managed to tell her father about the new co-ed track team. "It's the first year and the Y's are half-sponsors. Any high school can send one co-ed team to the big marathon in Buffalo in June. All you have to do is participate in six qualifying events. Don's a good runner and so am I. We have a chance to win . . ."

As she talked, her father made her a cup of tea. She noticed he didn't clean up the mess, though. Her father was cheerful and kind but he had a way of ignoring unpleasant chores. It never actually seemed to occur to him to clean anything.

When she finished talking, he said, "You worry too much, Little Mother."

"I have to worry about Tommy and the house," Laura defended herself between tears. She was sorry she'd said anything to her father. It wouldn't do any good.

"You're a good girl," he said. A sad look crossed his face. "You look so much like Gloria and you're already a thousand years older than she will ever be." He patted her hand and added, "That's beside the point. The point is that we can't allow some *femme fatale* to scoop up your Prince Charming. Join this wonderful track team. I'll get Mrs. Withers to come in and watch Tommy on Saturdays. She can do some of the cleaning for you too."

"We can't afford it," Laura said.

"You worry too much," her father said. Then he laughed and said, "I'll hock the family jewels or something. Seen my golf clubs?"

Laura helped her father find his clubs, made him a sandwich for lunch, and watched him as he drove away in his new Oldsmobile. *Why not hire someone?* she thought. *He's always got money for other things.* The minute she thought those things, she felt guilty. Her dad played golf because it was good for business. The new car was essential for his real estate business too.

Still, she was going to tell Don she'd be his partner when he called tonight. In his own way, her father had helped her understand that she must accept the offer. Between jokes, he'd kissed her lightly and said, "Don't let yourself be a loser, Laura. I lost the most important thing in the world because I didn't fight hard enough. Don't let that happen to you."

"I won't," she promised him, and she wouldn't. She was going to fight to have her own life — even if she did feel guilty.

CHAPTER 2

Laura couldn't help feeling shy as she walked into the cold, big gymnasium all alone. Most of the kids sitting on the bottom bleacher were familiar faces but none of them were exactly friends. There was something about walking across the empty room and across the basketball court to take a seat that made her feel as if everyone was looking at her. They *were* looking at her because she was directly in their line of vision, but she imagined that the inspection was critical and she would have liked to turn and run.

That's the White Rabbit talking, she reminded herself, as she tried to correct her posture and maintain her poise. It was funny, really, the way she hated those eyes on her. She knew she was better than average when it came to appearance. If she were honest, she would have to admit that she knew she was beautiful. A lot of people told her that, and she knew her mother had been beautiful, and she knew she looked a lot like Gloria. Actually, her self-conciousness had a lot to do with Gloria.

When she had been younger, children had been

cruel about her mother a couple of times. One had laughed and told her, "Your mother's a lush. My mother told me so." There weren't many incidents like that, but it didn't take many to terrify a bewildered fifth grader. *Your mother's a lush, but you're not your mother*, she reminded herself. She was halfway across the gym floor now and it wouldn't be long until she would be sitting safely with the others. Too bad Don had that dental appointment. When Don was with her she never felt frightened or alone.

Marilyn Rogers called to her and waved for her to come sit with her. Gratefully, Laura smiled at her and changed her direction a bit so she could join Marilyn. It was good to see a friendly face and Marilyn always seemed genuinely glad to see her.

She came to the bleacher and said, "Hi, Marilyn. I'm glad to see you."

Marilyn moved over a bit to give Laura room and asked, "Where's Don?"

"Dental appointment."

Marilyn nodded and said, "I talked poor Howie Golden into being my partner. He's not too happy about it but he's a good sort."

Laura asked, "Is he a good runner?"

Marilyn made a slight face and grinned. "He's got native talent but no drive. I've known Howie since kindergarten. In those days he wouldn't tie his shoes because he thought it was too much trouble."

"He went to Miss Merriweather's school with you?"

Marilyn nodded. "Same class for nine years.

Then I finally persuaded my mother to free me. I came to Central High and who's in my homeroom? Howie!"

Marilyn's laughter rang out across the near-empty gym. Several students looked over at her but she didn't seem the least bit uncomfortable. Laura wondered what it would be like to be that at ease. Marilyn seemed to have so much fun and so little worry. It must be great to live in a big house, have all that money, and look as good as she did. No wonder she was always so relaxed.

Marilyn said, "Maybe we can practice together some mornings. It would do Howie good to run with winners."

Laura nodded to say yes. How could she refuse? Yet she wasn't really keen on the idea of exposing herself to Marilyn's cheery disposition at six in the morning. Besides, she was sure that Marilyn was interested in Don, though she was beginning to understand that this girl was too open and friendly to be planning any attempts at taking Don away.

Marilyn nodded happily and said, "Good. I'm glad I found someone, even though I know that Howie hasn't got the drive to be a winner." She heaved a mock sigh and said, "Too bad. My mother would have loved for me to be a champion at something."

Laura smiled and pretended to understand. Marilyn's mother was one of the P.T.A. officers, so Laura knew what she was like — an assertive, determinedly cheerful woman who seemed to have all the awkward eagerness that Marilyn was missing. *At least her mother cares about her*, Laura thought, but she said nothing aloud. Marilyn would think she was self-pitying or silly if she said something like that.

In a way, it was good to realize that Marilyn could have problems of her own. Laura suddenly remembered that Marilyn wasn't very good in school. She'd ended up with C's in the two classes they shared last year. When she had transferred from that fancy prep school, they'd put her in honors, only to transfer her into the regular division after Thanksgiving.

When Marilyn asked, "How are you doing in history?" Laura was tempted to suggest they study together, but the coach began calling off names.

Marilyn was called first and she walked with such ease and cheerful eagerness up to the coach's table that Laura forgot all about offering to help her. Laura sat alone on the bench, tense and frightened again. In a minute, it would be her turn and she would have to walk in front of all those others one more time. She didn't like it and she wished Don could have come here to sign them up instead of her.

When the coach called, "Manning and Douglas," Laura walked stiffly over to the table. Coach Wilson looked up and said, "Hi, Laura. Where's your pal?"

"He had a dental appointment. Is it all right for me to sign for both of us?"

Coach Wilson nodded. "Good to have you here. You understand there are six qualifying meets. You must compete in all in order to be eligible for school champion team. The boy and girl team with top combined speed will go to Buffalo for the Northeastern Finals. You're on your own except for those six Saturdays." She handed Laura two parent waiver forms and said, "Give one to Don. You have your dad sign it and bring it in by Friday. OK?"

Laura's face burned as she took the paper. How did the coach know she lived with her father? This was Coach Wilson's first year at Central High so it had to be that other teachers had filled her in on the juicy gossip. Don was right. It *was* old news.

Laura turned and walked quickly toward the gym entrance. All she could think of was getting out of there as fast as she could go, so when Marilyn called out, "Wait, I thought we'd go get a Coke." Laura pretended she didn't hear her.

She kept right on walking until she got out of the gym and onto the sidewalk. Her face felt hot and her stomach was acting up again, so she was sure she'd be better off going home and starting supper for Tommy and her dad. At least the work would get her mind off the fact that her family was town gossip.

But Laura wasn't really able to forget her problems that evening, even though she kept busy. After she'd done the dishes and started on her homework, she found that she couldn't concentrate well. It seemed as though her mind kept replaying old scenes from the past. Soon she felt herself drifting off to the ugly night her mother left. She could almost see Gloria standing on the staircase, suitcase beside her, screaming at her father. Of course, neither adult knew that Laura was listening and watching everything that went on.

Neither of them knew that they shouted so

loudly they woke Tommy. Tommy was only seven then and Gloria was still calling him baby when she noticed him. That night, only Laura had comforted the boy, leading him back to his bedroom and singing to him after they heard the door close and their mother walk out into the black night. Since then, they'd seen Gloria a couple of times, had a dozen letters or postcards from her, then silence.

Laura gave up on her homework and went into the living room to watch television with Tommy. As she passed her father's bedroom, she heard him talking with someone. He said, "Friday night then, Love."

Who could he be talking to? Her heart skipped a beat — could it be Gloria on the telephone? Then she shook her head and smiled at her childishness. It was hardly Gloria he was calling love. He'd barely spoken her name in the two years since she left, and if Gloria called anyone it would be Tommy. She was not going to call her husband under any circumstances.

Laura didn't ask her father any questions when he came into the living room and said, "I have a date to show some property Friday evening. Think you and Don could babysit?"

"Sure," Laura answered. "We have the first track meet of the season the next day anyway. So we'd be coming in early."

She sent Tommy to bed and then went into her own room but couldn't sleep until two in the morning. Her mind was racing over the past, churning over the future, and there didn't seem to be anything she could do about it. Finally, she drifted off to sleep and it seemed just a few minutes before the alarm rang in the morning.

The next morning, Marilyn was waiting outside her house when Laura and Don ran by. They picked up Howie at the corner and the four runners jogged through that expensive neighborhood with big old houses and lawns that looked like meadows. Laura saw her first crocus of the season and she rejoiced in the emblem of spring.

Howie slowed them all down for the first couple of miles, then Marilyn said, "See you around," and started running faster. Don and Laura picked up their speed to keep pace with her. When they had left him a full block behind, Howie seemed to lose patience with bringing up the rear. He exerted himself to catch up after that; he kept the same pace.

When they returned home, they stopped for a minute in front of Howie's house. Laura said, "You're a good runner, Howie. You just need practice."

Howie smiled. "I need a wheelbarrow so Marilyn could give me a ride. I feel sorry for her."

Marilyn broke into a laugh. "Don't apologize. I needed a partner and you're the best available. I'm lucky." She turned and ran lightly down the street toward her own house. Laura and Don followed her.

Marilyn's hair hung down her shoulders in a heavy black cascade, spreading over the bright yellow jogging suit. Laura knew she had a different colored suit for each day of the week, but she was beginning to accept that the costumes were just part of being Marilyn Rogers. *She's nice,* Laura thought. *She's truly a nice person.* It no longer seemed important that she was probably interested in Don.

Glancing at Don, Laura told herself it couldn't really matter anyway. Don had been plain about his interest in her from the beginning. That first night, he'd said, "I want you to be my girl, Laurie. I want a good, steady thing. No boy gets girl, boy loses girl stuff. OK?"

Laura had nodded silently. She'd never dated anyone she felt was important in her life before, but she knew Don was going to be very, very important. He was everything she admired in a man — quiet, solid, steady, and trustworthy. Don would never lose his temper or run away from problems. Don was someone you could count on, and Laura wanted desperately to be able to count on someone.

They'd dated each other exclusively since that first evening. They ate lunch together at school, went out together on weekends, and studied together one or two nights a week. Her father made fun of Don sometimes, calling him "Dignified Don" or "Your Swain." Sometimes he complained that Don was so grown up he made him feel like an old man.

She was glad Don was the sort of person he was. After all, security was important in a relationship and if Don was a bit serious, so what? As far as Laura could see, life was no joke.

This morning, Don asked, "Get your history done?"

Laura nodded. "I'm going to be a straight A student if I hang around with you much longer."

Don smiled. "You *should* be a straight A student. I want you to get a scholarship so we can go to the University of Massachusetts together."

Laura's heart skipped a beat. Don was making plans for almost two years from now. He intended they would be together for a long time. A wonderful warmth flushed through her body at the thought of going to the same college as Don.

She shook her head and said, "Don't count chickens." She was thinking that when she graduated, Tommy would only be twelve. She would have to go to the community college or work. Laura thought grimly of the pile of unpaid bills on the counter at home.

She put her hand in Don's and smiled at him. He wasn't really handsome but that didn't matter. What mattered was that she felt safe around him. *He* would never run up bills. The minute the thought passed through her head, she felt guilty. How could she compare her father to Don? Her father had a lot of troubles that Don would never have.

She said, "See you in an hour."

Don kissed her lightly on the cheek and she went into her house. Her father was standing in the kitchen, drinking coffee. By the amused look on his face, Laura knew he'd been watching out the window. He said, "Good morning, Laura. Been frolicking with your beau?"

Laura tried to keep her face impassive as she poured herself a glass of milk. "Yes. Marilyn and Howie ran with us."

Her father nodded. "Couples. You looked like a real couple out there on the sidewalk."

"I saw a crocus this morning," Laura said. "Or the tip of a crocus to be more accurate."

"I'm not sure I like it," her father mused. "I'm not sure I like seeing that young man peck your cheek so early in the morning."

"I'm sixteen, Dad."

Her father shrugged, smiled, and poured himself another cup of coffee. "I know. I married your mother when she was a year older than you are right now. Maybe that's what scares me. Maybe I'm only jealous."

He was out of the room before Laura could think of anything to say to make him feel better. She worried about him all day long, at least partly because he seemed to be talking more about Gloria than ever before. She felt vaguely guilty about looking so much like her mother, knowing she was a constant reminder to him. Still, she couldn't help that, could she?

That evening, her dad didn't come home for dinner and Laura invited Don over for pizza. They were watching television when Don asked, "Where did your father go?"

Though she really didn't believe it, she gave him the reason her father had told her. "He's showing a house to some customers."

At ten-thirty, Don said, "Your dad's customers sure do like the dark." He was smiling.

"What are you thinking?" Laura asked.

"I'm thinking your dad's probably got a girl."

"Maybe," Laura nodded. That made sense. The phone call and even talking so much about Gloria would fit. Maybe he was finally getting over her mother. "I'd like to think so," Laura said.

"Why did she leave?" Don asked.

"Gloria? She left because she was a drunk."

"But lots of drunks stay home," Don probed gently.

Laura was grateful that Don hadn't been more inquisitive than he was. She realized that he'd asked because of a concern for her. She tried to tell him the truth without getting into the awful details. "My mother married very young and I guess she thought she missed a lot. At least, when she drank, she'd cry about not having had a chance to enjoy life. She was beautiful and my dad was jealous. They had horrible fights. Then, she got so ashamed. She used to wake me in the middle of the night to apologize. I guess she decided it was time to move on. Last I heard, she was a hostess in a fancy hotel in Boston."

Don put his arm around Laura and kissed her protectively. "Poor Laurie. And ever since, you've been taking care of your dad and Tommy."

Laura jumped up and said, "Popcorn needs salt. Subject needs changing." She was moved by Don's praise but didn't want his pity. She could not afford pity.

When Don said good night, he held her tight and kissed her again, saying, "We've got a big day tomorrow."

Laura nodded. "I hope we win."

He held her close for a minute and said, "We're already winners. See you at six."

Laura was asleep before her father came in at twelve, but she woke when she heard him whistling in the kitchen. When she woke the second time at two, she thought it was funny that her dad was still awake. Then she realized that it was her brother calling her that had awakened her. She found him sitting on the side of his bed, rocking to and fro as he called her. He looked up at her and said, "Laurie, I'm awful sick."

Tommy was running a fever and he had been sick enough to vomit into the trash can beside his bed. Laura patted his arm, said, "Good kid, Tommy. Don't worry." She quickly changed his pajamas, cleaned up the room, and brought him some water.

His temperature was only a hundred, so he probably wasn't too sick, Laura thought as she went back to her own bed. If she was lucky, she could still get enough sleep to win at the meet tomorrow.

But she wasn't lucky. Within thirty minutes, Tommy was calling to her again. This time, she was able to help him to the bathroom but he felt so awful that he insisted she stay by his side. Laura took his temperature a second time and discovered it was climbing.

At three-thirty, Laura tried to leave Tommy long enough to get her father, but he held on to her hand tightly and cried for his mother. When he fell asleep at four, she tried to slip out of the room but he was wide awake immediately. She said, "I'm just going for Daddy."

Her father got up and walked into Tommy's bedroom, felt his forehead, said, "Good girl," to Laura and went back to bed. Laura stared help-lessly at the clock and felt the tears rise in her eyes. She would be in no state to run tomorrow even if Tommy let her go, and Tommy showed no inclination to let her go.

The worst of it was that if she didn't make that meet tomorrow, she would be out of the whole season. She could call Don and he could get Marilyn to run with him, but that would make them permanent partners. Of course, Marilyn would be delighted and Howie would be happy to be off the hook. She supposed she owed it to Don to call him so he could participate, but she would have given just about anything to let it slide.

It was silly to even think that way, Laura knew. She had no real choice. Tommy was more important than any race, and she had to let Don know what was going on. To let him get to the starting point without her would be cruel. Laura sighed and patted Tommy gently on the back. He was sleeping in small spurts, then waking as his stomach acted up again and again. Tommy looked at her and asked, "Will you stay with me?"

Laura smiled at him and said, "Of course."

Tommy seemed to relax a bit and he whispered, "Laurie, tell me something."

It was an old ritual which they'd begun during those last months when Gloria's bouts of drinking got so bad. Laura would lead Tommy into his bedroom and begin by saying, "Now I'm going to tell you something."

Laura laughed. "First I have to call someone. Then I'll come back and tell you a something story."

Tommy smiled and said, "Thanks, Laura."

Within five minutes, Laura was back in Tommy's room. She smiled brightly, trying to forget the disdain in Don's voice as he had asked, "What's wrong with your father?"

She didn't have to explain her decisions to Don or anyone else. She knew what was important, and Tommy was important — more important than a track meet. She brushed his hair away from his hot forehead and asked, "Where shall we begin?"

"Begin at the beginning," Tommy answered promptly. "Once upon a time . . ."

CHAPTER   3

Tommy slept off and on all day, but his temperature stayed high and he couldn't keep any
food down. About three, Laura called the doctor
and asked to bring him in. "I'll get a cab," Laura
said.

"Your father working?" Doctor Thomas asked.

"Yes," Laura answered. "I thought he would be
home by now but you know how the real estate
business is. I can never count on regular hours."

Doctor Thomas sighed loudly. "You're on my
way home, Laura. I'll be there in an hour."

The first thing the doctor did was take Laura's
temperature when he got there.

"I'm not sick," she protested.

"Don't talk with a thermometer in your mouth,"
Dr. Thomas teased. "Besides, you'd be the last one
to know if you were sick. How's the stomach?"

"Better," she answered. When he took the
thermometer out of her mouth, she added, "Jogging helped."

Doctor Thomas nodded and went over to
Tommy's bed. As he pressed on Tommy's
stomach, asking where it hurt, he said to Laura,

"Could be the jogging that helped. Could be the new love in your life."

Laura blushed. "How did you know about Don?" she asked.

"Pittsfield is a small town," he answered. "Besides, you run by my house every morning just about the time I'm having my first cup of coffee. Where's your young man today?"

The old hurt returned to Laura. She felt her stomach contract and she didn't know what to say. Certainly, she didn't feel like telling the doctor that her boyfriend was running in a track meet without her. She asked, "Is Tommy going to be sick long?"

Doctor Thomas shrugged. "Can't tell. Some of this stuff going around moves into the chest. Most stays in the stomach. Give him these pills and keep him in bed. Bring him in on Tuesday. You should have a check-up too."

"I'm really fine."

"You're in pain right now." The doctor laughed aloud at her obvious dismay. "No, I'm not psychic, Laura. I've just learned to read body language. When I asked where your boyfriend was, you bent over and folded your arms across your stomach. A sure sign the irritation isn't completely gone. Where is he?"

Laura forced herself to smile. "Nothing serious, Doctor. I was going to a track meet with Don and some other kids. When Tommy got sick, I had to stay home. It's all right, really."

Doctor Thomas nodded and patted Tommy on the forehead, then patted Laura on the shoulder. "You're a good girl," he said.

Laura felt tears sting her eyes as she watched the doctor leave the bedroom. Why did she want to cry because he praised her? What was wrong with her? Maybe she was crazy instead of sick.

Laura didn't have time to worry about herself for long because Tommy was restless and kept calling for different things. When she tried to persuade him to nap, he said, "I feel better."

At lunch, Laura made Tommy some toast and soup and this time he was able to keep it down. But as he got slightly better, he became more and more restless. She had hoped that when his fever went down she would be able to get some of her schoolwork done, but Tommy seemed to sense when she even began to think of leaving. He opened his eyes and demanded, "Don't go, Laurie."

Laura bent down, brushed his forehead, and smiled down at him. He looked so sweet and young. She said, "No, of course not."

Tommy opened his sleepy blue eyes wide and said, "You're good to me, Laurie. When Mama comes home, I'll tell her you took good care of me."

For a minute, Laura was alarmed. Could Tommy's fever be so high he was getting delirious? But when she shook down the thermometer and stuck it in his mouth, she was careful not to let Tommy know she was worried. She said, "Just a check-up, Tommy Tiger."

His temperature was close to normal. Tommy wasn't delirious and he wasn't teasing. Somewhere, deep down in his heart, he still believed that Gloria was returning.

"You really believe she's coming back, don't you?" Laura asked.

"I know she is," Tommy answered. "She's been on a long journey, just like Dorothy and Alice and Gerda."

Laura kept her voice soft as she responded. "I guess you mean Dorothy from Oz and Alice from Wonderland, but who is Gerda?"

"You know," Tommy replied crossly. "She's the one who went to see the Snow Queen."

Laura nodded. "All of those people are characters in books, Tommy. They're not real."

Tommy shifted impatiently. "I know they're fake but you were the one who told me real and fake characters were just the same."

Laura laughed out loud and kissed Tommy's damp forehead. "It was my English term paper that I read to you, wasn't it?"

"Don't laugh, Laura." Tommy looked as though he might begin to cry as he insisted, "She's coming back."

Laura patted him on the shoulder and softened her voice. "Tommy Tiger, I read you a term paper that said characters in stories and people in real life are more alike than most folks think. It was a big idea for a little boy. You've just got to believe me — Gloria is not a princess in a fairy tale and she isn't coming back."

Tommy turned his back to Laura, crumpled his body into a round ball and buried his head in the pillow. Laura thought, *Poor kid, he misses her so much.*

Laura waited, hoping Tommy would go back to sleep. She leafed through her history book, reading the chapter headings but not being able to bear to actually read the text. The Industrial Revolution seemed so remote and unimportant. Still, a scholarship to the University of Massachusetts *was* important.

Instead of daydreaming, I should be studying, she told herself. She took a deep breath and made a conscious effort to begin reading. She was on the second page when Tommy turned back to her. He said, "She'll be back as soon as she gets return fare."

"What do you mean?" Laura asked.

"Remember the time Mama was gone so long? Daddy had to go after her because she didn't have return fare."

Laura laughed bitterly. The month before she left for good, Gloria had stayed away three times. Each time, she had claimed she'd gone shopping and spent all her money — that she didn't have return fare from Boston. *My mother was like a child*, Laura thought. *She couldn't help herself*.

Laura said, "Let's change the subject, OK? Let's talk about your scout trip. Where are we going?"

Tommy answered, "We haven't decided. We're going to Mystic or Sturbridge."

"Which would you like?" Laura prompted.

"I want Mystic where there are ships but some of the guys want Sturbridge. We vote at the next meeting."

Laura smiled at Tommy. He was a sweet little boy and today he seemed younger than his nine years. Funny about Tommy, but the more grown-up he talked, the more vulnerable he seemed. *He needs me*, Laura thought. She felt a warm flush of love rush in to cover the resentment and anger she'd been feeling about being left at home.

"I want to go where you want to go," Laura said loyally.

"I wish I could talk to Mama. I'd ask her where she wants to go."

"What do you mean?"

"We're supposed to ask our mothers where they want to go," Tommy explained.

"Then you have to ask *me*," Laura said. "I vote for whatever you want."

Tommy shook his head. "But what if Mama wants to see the ships and I vote for the other?"

"Tommy, your mother is gone. You'd better accept that!" Even as she said the words, she wished she hadn't spoken so sharply. She didn't want to make Tommy feel worse than he already did.

Tears ran down Tommy's face and he said, "You're mean. You don't want Mama to come back, but she will. Wait and see."

"Tom Manning, you've got to face facts. Your mother is gone for good. She went off and left us and I'm stuck taking care of you. Now sometimes we just have to accept things we don't like. It's a fact of life, Tommy . . ." Laura stopped.

Tommy's thin little body was heaving as though it was being shaken by a giant hand. He turned his face to the wall, buried his head in his hands, and would not look at Laura.

Laura watched helplessly. Those first few months after Gloria left, there had been scenes like this more than once, but that was almost two years ago. Laura was dismayed to realize that

Tommy still believed so strongly. *Time doesn't heal wounds*, Laura thought bitterly. *It just covers them over.*

She reached out and touched Tommy on the shoulder. "Don't cry, Tommy. I'm sorry. I really am."

But Tommy only pushed farther into his pillow and said, "Go away," through muffled sobs. Laura stood up and said, "All right, I'll go start dinner. If you want me, just call me." She hated the "poor-me" sound of her own voice but she didn't know what to do about it.

I guess I really do feel sorry for myself, Laura thought. *It just seems as though I can't win. I stay home to take care of Tommy and Don's mad at me. By the middle of the first day, Tommy's mad at me too. All I need is for Dad to come in the door. Bet I could pick a fight with him too.*

Laura made the salad and put the chicken in the oven before she peeked into Tommy's room again. He was asleep. Relieved that he was getting some rest, she did the laundry while she waited for her dad to come home. She was also hoping that Don would call when he got home from the meet.

At six, her dad phoned to say he'd be out late, so Laura put supper on a tray and carried it to Tommy's room. Tommy was awake and there were dark circles under his eyes. He looked accusingly at Laura but said nothing.

They watched television for a while after dinner and things were easier between them. Laura kept looking at her watch, wondering why Don didn't call. Was he really mad at her? She also wondered where her father was. Did he have another date? It wasn't like him to stay away without calling.

When Don called at seven-thirty, he sounded fine. He said, "Marilyn and I came in with third total points so we're in the running."

Laura forced herself to sound cheerful as she asked, "Was Howie disappointed?"

Don laughed. "Delighted, I guess. At least that's what Marilyn said."

Laura waited for Don to ask about Tommy. Instead, he asked, "Want to go to the movies tonight?"

"Can't. My dad's not home."

"Figures," Don said.

"Don't be that way, Don," Laura said. "My dad works very hard to take care of us."

"And you work very hard to take care of your dad," Don snapped. "I'm sorry, Laurie. It's just that I thought we had it all worked out, and then it turned out we didn't have anything worked out at all."

Laura didn't know what else to say. She felt silly, defending her father to her boyfriend. She was annoyed that Don *still* hadn't asked about Tommy. Finally, when the silence seemed too heavy and too long, she asked, "Want to come over? Watch television?"

"I'm tired, I guess. I'll stay home unless you really want me?"

Now Laura did feel annoyed. If she hadn't really wanted him, she wouldn't have asked. Would she? What was wrong with Don this evening? She said, "Do what you want to."

"You don't sound too cheerful. I guess you're tired too. How's Tommy?"

Somehow, the fact that Don asked now, upset Laura more than ever. She said, "Fine." At that moment, her father walked in the door but she didn't feel like telling Don. He probably didn't want to see her and if he knew her dad was home, he might feel impelled to keep their date. She said, "Tommy's calling. I have to hang up."

"See you Monday," Don said. Don could never be with her on Sunday because he visited his grandfather in Springfield. He lived with his mother and great-aunt, and Laura had no idea where his real father was. In fact, she didn't know much about Don's family at all. And she was sure he didn't want to tell her. Since Laura didn't like to talk about her mother, she was careful to respect Don's need for privacy.

Laura put the phone on the hook and turned to follow her father into the kitchen. At least she would have a chance to talk with him about Tommy. Maybe it was just as well that Don didn't come over.

When she got into the kitchen, her father was eating cold chicken. She said, "There's gravy and vegetables. All you have to do is heat them." Why *did* she sound so accusing all the time?

If her father noticed the nagging in her voice, he ignored it as he answered, "Too much trouble."

Laura sat down beside her father and said, "I want to talk to you about Tommy. He's got this whole fantasy worked out about Gloria. Latest thing is, he's sure she's coming back as soon as she gets return fare."

Her father shook his head and said, "Kids are something, aren't they?"

"Will you talk with him, Dad? It isn't good for him to believe the impossible."

Her father nodded his head and said, "I'll tell him that dreams don't always come true. But some do — you know that, don't you?"

Somehow, the light-hearted twinkle in her father's eye was all she needed to rouse her anger. "It's not fair to me, Dad. He uses Gloria against me whenever he doesn't want to do something. I want him to grow up to face responsibility — to be reliable."

"Not like your old man," her father finished. "All right, Little Mother, I'll talk with him. But sometimes dreams are good things to have."

Laura looked steadily at her father. Then she shook her head in mock exasperation. "You're not much older than Tommy in a lot of ways, you know that?"

"And you're as old as the hills, you know that?" her father teased.

Laura felt better after her talk with her father, and she was able to get a lot of homework done. Tommy would recover soon and she would see Don on Monday. *Things will be better,* she promised herself.

Yet, there were things about the day that frightened her. Tommy seemed so determined to believe that Gloria was coming home. She could see that her father wasn't going to be much help with that one. Although she loved him very much, Laura knew she had been right when she accused him of not being much older than Tommy.

As for Don, things would probably straighten out. He would just have to accept her as she was — and that included her responsibilities to Tommy. Though she had always been proud of the fact that Don was as solid and trustworthy as anyone could be, she could not ignore the disdain in his voice when he spoke of her father. Laura didn't like that. Could Don be jealous of Tommy and her dad?

Laura turned off her lights and went to sleep, but thirty minutes later she was wide awake, feeling sorry for herself again. She had just realized that none of them, not Tommy, nor her father, nor Don, had asked her anything at all about herself. Not one of them had asked, "How are you" or "How was your day?" Wasn't she important too?

CHAPTER 4

Sunday went so fast for Laura that she hardly noticed it at all. Instead of clearing up as she had hoped, Tommy's virus got worse and Laura spent the night and day with him. He had a high fever, so she slept in the armchair beside his bed.

She was too tired to get up in time to run with Don. When she came downstairs at seven-thirty, her father said, "Stay home, Laura. You should sleep."

"I can't," she protested. "I have a test on the Industrial Revolution."

"You can make it up."

"Dad! You always think things are so easy. Even if I get a note from you, this teacher will give me a test three times harder for makeup."

"OK, Little Mother, I guess your way is the best. You're going to amount to something, not be like your old man."

Laura leaned her head against her father's shoulder and felt a moment of peace. She shook her head and said, "I'm sorry if I'm cross."

"That's my girl. And don't worry about the test. You'll probably make a hundred."

Taking a test on the Industrial Revolution would have been hard enough on a regular Monday, Laura thought, but it was going to be doubly tough today. She hoped the brisk walk to school would refresh her, and she deliberately left her jacket at home even though it was a cool spring morning. A block from the house, Laura began jogging and that felt better. By the time she turned the corner of the block where the school was, she almost had the cobwebs erased from her brain.

Bouncing up the steps two-by-two, Laura felt good again. After all, she had a wonderful family, a wonderful boyfriend, and she had herself. Most of the time, Laura liked herself just fine and she suspected that as time went on, she would learn to accept her situation more gracefully. After all, she wasn't the only one with problems.

On the edge of that thought, Marilyn called out to her. "Hi Laura, did you hear we placed?" She joined Laura as they walked down the hall toward their lockers. Marilyn answered herself, "Of course you heard. How was the movie?"

"We didn't go," Laura said briefly. The good mood vanished as quickly as if some giant hand had brushed away the sunshine and trailed fog into its place.

"Didn't go?" Marilyn asked. "Is your brother worse?"

'Well, he's not any better," Laura said. At least Marilyn had asked about Tommy. That was more than Don had done. Laura asked, "See you at lunch?"

Marilyn nodded and shivered. "If I'm still alive.

I've got Higgens's test on the Industrial Revolution third period."

"I've got him right now — first."

"Oh wow! I wonder if he'll give both classes the same test? Listen, Laura, I don't suppose . . ." Marilyn stopped herself and laughed. "No, I don't suppose you would and I don't blame you. I'll just have to do my best."

There was a slight edge in Marilyn's voice and Laura wondered if Marilyn was imitating her mother. Laura said, "You'll do fine."

Marilyn laughed and shrugged helplessly. "I'll see you at lunch."

"Sure," Laura agreed. She was hoping Marilyn would leave now, because Don was coming down the hall. If Marilyn noticed Don, she pretended she didn't and walked away quickly.

Don's first words were, "What happened to you? I waited on the corner this morning for twenty minutes."

"Oh Don, I thought you'd know I couldn't jog with you," Laura said.

"We jog every day except Sunday. Has that changed?" Don asked.

Laura shook her head. "Nothing's changed. It's just that I was so tired."

Don reached out and touched her chin, lifting her face to the light. He said, "You look awful. Didn't you get any sleep?"

It would have been nice to know that Don cared enough about her to be concerned, except his voice sounded so angry. She said, "You don't sound very sympathetic."

"I'm not," Don said shortly. "You're going to

have to learn sometime that you can't do everything for them."

"And you've got to learn that my family life is none of your business." Laura choked out before she ran away, clutching her books in front of her as though they were a shield protecting her from an invisible enemy.

When Don didn't call or come after her, Laura ran even faster. As she rounded the corner, she collided with the tiny art teacher who was known for her creative teaching, brilliant watercolors, and sharp tongue. Horrendous Hunter, she was sometimes called.

For one second as she was falling, Laura hoped to avoid crashing on top of the tiny woman but she was not lucky enough to keep from the inevitable. To make things worse, two other students rounded the corner as the homeroom bell rang and tripped over them.

The art teacher began shrieking, "I'm ruined! I'm ruined! Look at this!"

Laura scrambled to her feet, tried to help Ms. Hunter up, but the older woman shrieked, "You deliberately tripped me. You nasty girl!"

Laura saw it was no good trying to apologize. She stared at the red and purple paint that was running all over the floor. When the vice principal arrived and led them both to the office, Laura could do no more than say, "I'm sorry."

It occurred to her later that she might have said that Ms. Hunter was on the wrong side of the hallway. It also occurred to her that she'd never been in trouble before, while Ms. Hunter had a major altercation with someone nearly every day.

However, Laura didn't try to defend herself and she accepted the two nights detention meekly before she rushed to her first-period class.

She was fifteen minutes late and the test had already begun. When she took her paper and sat down, it took a minute to recognize the questions, she was so upset. The hysterical scene with Ms. Hunter, on top of the quarrel with Don, on top of being so tired, was more than she could bear. She wanted to get up and walk out of the room. *Dad was right*, she thought. *I should have stayed in bed.*

Some of the test questions asked things she'd never studied and some seemed ambiguous to her. She raced through the exam, answering the ones she was sure of first; then she went back and studied the unclear ones carefully. Five minutes before the bell, she still had seven blank spaces on her paper. She took a deep breath and marked what seemed to her to be the best guesses.

Laura felt exhausted, discouraged, and shattered by the time she left history class and went into English. *At least I'll be able to rest,* she thought when she saw the film projector. Apparently Mr. Whitman had ordered another movie. He believed that film was the literature of the future and never missed a chance to run any movie that was vaguely connected with the curriculum.

Two minutes after the projector started, Laura was asleep. When she woke, Mr. Whitman was standing beside her. He looked very angry as he said, "Come with me."

The bell rang for third period and students poured out into the hallways. For the second time in less than two hours, Laura was following a teacher to the vice principal's office. *It can't be real*, Laura told herself. *It's like a nightmare or something.*

She was shivering when she entered the vice principal's office. He said what Laura had been thinking. "This isn't real."

He listened as Mr. Whitman complained about Laura's inattention for a few minutes and then he interrupted, "Thank you, Mr. Whitman. You go on back to class. I'll take care of this."

As soon as the teacher left, the vice principal said, "Now how can I get hold of your father? You're obviously tired and you need to go home and rest."

"No detention?" Laura asked.

The vice principal shook his head. "I know you're a good student, Laura. If you fall asleep in school, it's because you're tired. Right?"

She nodded her head gratefully. "My father is home today. The number is 445-9078."

The vice principal said as he dialed, "Now go sit in the chair outside my office until he gets here. Try not to snore."

Laura managed a small smile but she really didn't think it was funny. Nor did she think it was funny when her father came into the office and asked in a jolly voice, "How's my juvenile delinquent today?"

Before she could answer, the secretary stepped up to the counter and said, "Mr. Manning? Mr. Wilson would like to talk with you."

Her dad was gone more than a minute and when

he came back he looked troubled. It seemed strange to Laura to see his unlined and youthful face creased and worried-looking. She asked, "Is anything wrong?"

Her father shook his head and said, "Come on, Little Mother. Let's take you home and put you to bed."

In the car, she asked again, "Dad, what did the vice principal say to you? Why do you look like that?"

He smiled again and shook his head, tossing his longish brown hair around. "Look funny, did I? I thought that I was doing a proper imitation of a concerned father."

Laura laughed. "It was a horrible morning. You were right. I should have stayed home. I knocked down the art teacher, fought with Don, and probably flunked history as well as fell asleep in class. All within two and a half hours." Though she knew it was worth the effort, it was hard to keep the tears out of her voice. "Isn't that a riot?" she asked.

"Sounds tragic to me," her father said.

Laura turned to look at her father. She said, "You're taking it seriously."

Her father shook his head in agreement. "Your Mr.-What's-His-Name read me the riot act. He said I was taking advantage of you and treating you wrong. I'm sorry, Laurie."

"Oh, Dad, I'm sorry," Laura said. Now she felt guilty about her father on top of her other problems, she thought grimly.

He patted her knee. "Didn't think I'd tell you

this until it was more definite, Laura, but I think I've got some wonderful news. It's in the future, of course. Maybe a few weeks or months . . ."

Laura watched as her father's face lit up again. She thought she knew what he would be promising her — a full time housekeeper. He'd promised her that off and on ever since Gloria left. Well, it was a nice thought. She yawned. It would be good to get home and get to bed. She could probably play sick tomorrow and then she could worry about all her problems on Wednesday. *Let Wednesday take care of Wednesday*, she thought. What was he saying?

". . . and so we're in communication again. I've talked to her on the phone a dozen times and been out there once. Of course, she's been through a lot." His face clouded over a moment.

"Who?" Laura asked. Her blood seemed to be slowing down. She seemed to be getting very, very cold.

"She looks older, of course. She's still beautiful, though. And she wants to come back. At least, she thinks she wants to come back. So that it looks as though things may work out very well after all."

"Gloria wants to come back?" Laura asked. She hoped her hearing didn't freeze before she got the answer. She was really getting very cold all over.

"Now, don't count on it, but yes. I think I can say definitely that she's coming back. Won't that be wonderful?" He looked expectantly at his daughter.

"No," Laura said precisely, clearly, and distinctly through numb lips. "No."

Her father looked surprised, then frightened. "Now, Laura, it won't be like before. She's sober. Maybe you didn't understand, but she's been sober for a month now. She's at this treatment center called Serenity Farm where they help alcoholics. She's getting well."

Laura said nothing else to her father. How could she tell him how she felt? What could she say to explain the anger and fear this news brought? After two years — what right did Gloria have to come back into their lives? How could she throw all of her family away and then come back like that? How could she dare? Did she think Tommy and she were disposable children?

When the car pulled into the driveway, she said, "Thank you for picking me up. I think I'll take a nap. I'm very tired."

Her father tried to kiss her but she pulled away. For a minute, she thought he would try again to persuade her that it was wonderful Gloria wanted to come back. He said, "Little Mother . . ."

"My name is Laura. Please call me that."

"All right, Laura. Go to bed. You're shivering. I'm sorry you're so upset but you don't want to get sick."

"Yes, I feel very cold." Laura walked up to her own room.

CHAPTER 5

Laura slept through Monday and saw her father for only a few minutes on Tuesday. It was Wednesday evening before they got a chance to talk again.

He began by asking, "Did your friends at school miss you?"

"No one said anything."

"Still upset, Laura?"

She tried to maintain her frozen calmness as she said, "I'd rather not talk about it. I'd also rather you not say anything to Tommy about this. Gloria was never noted for her dependability."

Her father frowned. "Your mother has been very sick for a long time. She hasn't been herself. On Saturday, you'll see a new Gloria. You'll feel better."

A sick feeling hit Laura in the pit of her stomach. She slammed the cupboard door and began mopping the enamel sink furiously. Her voice was choked as she asked, "Is she coming here Saturday?"

Her father shook his head. "No, of course not.

We all have a lot of work to do before she can stay here. And she needs to stay at the Farm for a while."

When Laura said nothing, her father continued. "We're going to visit her at Serenity Farm Saturday."

"You're going to visit her. I have to study."

"This isn't like you, Laura. You sound so — tough."

"Do I? Well, it is about time I got a little tougher, isn't it?" Laura looked around the kitchen to see if everything was done.

As she watered the geraniums, her father said, "You should come with us. It will be a beginning."

"I have to study." Laura was aware of a vague sense of exultation, even though she was feeling so upset. At least he was pleading with her, for once.

"I hope you'll change your mind," her father said. He sounded tired and worried. "Tommy and I will leave at nine."

Laura realized she was frightening her father by her coldness, but she didn't know any other way to behave. She felt so many things at once, but the main emotion was numb pain. *If I show how betrayed I feel, I'll break down and that won't help*, she thought. Out loud, she said, "I think it is wrong to take Tommy. He could be so hurt. He wants his mother so much, but the mother he wants is a fantasy."

"Gloria wants to see him too," her father answered.

"You're the parent. It's your decision."

"Laura, I know you love Tommy . . ."

"I have to study, Dad." Laura folded the towels neatly over the rack and went to her room. Once there, she opened her history book and began rereading the chapter on the beginning of the labor movement. She felt so sick and miserable that she would have liked to go to bed and stay there, but she couldn't afford to do that. This time, she reminded herself, she would have to make an A on the quiz to balance the C-plus she'd made on the last one. She couldn't afford any more mistakes.

That was exactly the way Laura felt about every aspect of her life that week — that she had to be very careful. Everything she did seemed to be difficult and every friendship she had seemed to be in danger. Though she chose her words carefully, things got worse and worse. In spite of the frozen caution which she felt, she seemed to do all the wrong things.

Though Don and she ran together on Wednesday morning, it wasn't the same. Laura resented his interference in her family life, and at the same time she found that Marilyn's irrepressible energy annoyed her. On Thursday, after three miles, she was in such a bad mood that she pretended to be overtired. She panted, "You two go on. I'm going to turn around."

"We'll go too," Marilyn said cheerfully.

Laura shook her head stubbornly. "You're training. Keep going. I'll see you at school."

"Oh, Laura, if you don't feel well, we'll come back with you," Marilyn said. "After all, it's clear that we're already champions. Right, Don?"

Don didn't answer Marilyn but he asked Laura, "Are you sick?"

Laura shook her head. Why did she feel like crying again? She said, "I guess I'm just worn out. I'll see you later."

"You're supposed to run every morning. Dr. Thomas said so." Don's voice was gentle.

Somehow, the tone of his voice made her more irritable than ever. She said, "I *have* run. See you." She turned away from them and started jogging toward her home.

Though Marilyn called out, "Laura, wait," neither she nor Don followed her.

Nothing seemed to go right that day. The books she needed for her history report were all checked out and the film projector broke down in English. One of the kids said, "At least Laura will stay awake now."

The whole class laughed at the memory of Laura falling asleep. Mr. Whitman turned the lights on and Laura's face burned red. Kelton Kott, who sat two seats in front of her, leaned over and said, "Don't let it get to you, Laura. They are boors."

Laura smiled gratefully at Kelton and opened her book to the poem they were supposed to read. She didn't know Kelton very well but she did know that Marilyn Rogers dated him at the beginning of the year. Kids said it crushed Marilyn when Kelton dropped her.

What kind of a person could crush the irrepressible Marilyn? Laura sneaked a look at Kelton. He was handsome and over six feet tall and maybe that was part of his attraction. If you were as tall as Marilyn, a fellow who is taller was a rare find. Besides his appearance, Kelton was a straight A student, but she didn't know much else about him. He didn't seem to have many friends, but then neither did she.

Laura smiled at Kelton and he smiled back. Then she turned her attention to her English lesson. Though she was still doing well in school, it seemed to take a lot more energy to keep her mind on the job at hand. Every few minutes she would find her thoughts straying back to her family.

Tommy would see Gloria tomorrow. What would it be like? Would it upset him terribly? What would happen if Gloria began drinking again? Laura couldn't get the memory of her mother's distraught face out of her mind. Every time she thought of Gloria, she thought of her standing at the bottom of the stairs that last night. She could still see the tears on her mother's swollen face as she cried out, "I'm leaving you! You'll never have to be bothered with me again!"

Now, Laura shivered at the horrible memories and picked up her books to leave English. The bell had rung. Class was over and she'd wasted the whole period worrying. Don, her father, and Doctor Thomas were all right. She did worry too much, but how did you keep from worrying?

On the way out of class, Kelton Kott caught up with Laura and asked, "Would you be interested in studying together tonight? We could meet at the library."

Laura was so startled she stared at him. Didn't

he know she was dating Don? Maybe he just wanted to study because they were both good students. She said, "I'm going to the library about six. We could spend an hour or so on English, but I have a history report I'm *really* worried about."

Kelton smiled again and Laura couldn't help being pleased he'd asked her. It was kind of nice to think that someone as handsome as Kelton was interested in her. At the same time, she felt vaguely guilty about disloyalty to Don. Still, he'd only asked her to study with him — not to marry him.

Kelton said, "I hope you know you're the first student at Central High I've ever asked to study with me." Then he made a mock face of horror. "Judging from what I've encountered, you'll probably be the only one."

Laura smiled and said, "See you tonight. I have to meet Don for lunch." That would tell him that she was still dating Don in case he didn't know. No sense letting him get the wrong idea.

Kelton raised his eyebrows and said, "Oh yes, Don Douglas."

Laura had no idea what that was supposed to mean. Her stomach was hurting again and she wanted to get to the cafeteria to get some milk and lunch before it got really painful. Since she'd learned about Gloria's return to their lives, the pain was almost as bad as it had been in the beginning.

Laura felt helpless to explain why the thought of her mother's return was almost as upsetting as the abandonment had been. She knew she ought to be glad her mother wasn't drinking anymore.

She knew she ought to be glad that Tommy was going to get his mother back and her father was going to get his wife, but all she could feel was anger. Most of the time, she tried not to worry, but it didn't do much good.

She dreaded the day when she would have to face Gloria for the first time. She'd avoided going to Serenity Farm, but soon Gloria would be coming home. *Don't think about that now*, she warned herself. *Think of lunch.*

When she found Don in the cafeteria, he was talking and laughing with Marilyn and Evelyn. They were so busy among themselves that Laura stood with her tray in her hands, waiting for someone to give her room at the table for just a fraction too long. By the time Don noticed her and scooted over, she was feeling stiff and miserable. It seemed as though she was spending a lot of time being unhappy lately. *The White Rabbit better slow down*, she told herself.

Don asked, "Do you want to go with us to pick out track suits this afternoon?"

She shook her head. "No. I'm not on the team and it would be sort of silly."

"Come on," Marilyn urged. "Your company is always welcome."

Laura turned to stare at her. Why did Marilyn feel she needed to say that? It was as if she and Don were the couple and Laura was the outsider. For a while, she'd almost liked Marilyn, but now she was sure that her first guess was right. Marilyn Rogers was really after Don all along. *Well, let her have him*. Laura thought.

"I said no."

Marilyn realized that something was wrong because she nudged Evelyn and said, "Let's go. We have that thing to study."

Evelyn looked sort of surprised but she got up dutifully and followed Marilyn out of the cafeteria. Laura was sure it hurt the plump girl to leave her dessert behind.

Don said, "You could be polite. Marilyn's done nothing to you."

"You talk like a ninety-year-old man. Say what you mean." Laura was close to tears again. Her stomach hurt and she wished the bell would ring so she could get out of there.

Don pushed his carton of milk around on the tray. He said, "Laura, you're getting to be impossible. You snap at your friends, fall asleep in class, you pick fights with me. What's wrong?"

"She's your friend, not mine!" Laura cried.

"Are you jealous of Marilyn?" Don asked. "Don't be. I thought we agreed. . . ."

"We didn't agree about anything, Don Douglas. You told me! Now I guess you're free to tell me something else."

"What is wrong with you? Is it your dad?"

"No. It's not my dad. Stay out of my family life."

Don stood up and said, "Laura, when we started dating, I told you I couldn't stand quarreling. I can't. I've got a lot of other things to do. See you tomorrow."

"No. Not tomorrow. We're over, Don." The minute she said those words, she felt sick. She wanted to take them back but she couldn't. It was as though a new, hateful Laura was in control.

Don looked at her for a minute and then he said, "If you change your mind, let me know. I've got to get to class. You too."

He walked away and Laura realized that he'd taken her seriously. It was as simple as that — Don was gone from her life. The cafeteria was empty and she was late for class.

If she had been worried in the morning, she was really upset in the afternoon. Why had she picked a fight with Don? And why had Don walked away like that? Why couldn't he understand that she was just in a bad mood.

Laura spent the rest of the school day hoping Don would seek her out so she could explain. . . . But what would she explain? There was nothing to say, really.

The worst of it was that Don didn't try to talk with her. She didn't even see him from a distance. Suddenly, it was as if he'd been swallowed up by Central High. Hundreds of kids walked past her as classes changed, but nowhere could Laura see even a glimpse of Don Douglas's bright red hair. *He'll call after school*, she promised herself.

He didn't call, and when she met Kelton at the library at six-thirty, he asked her to go to a party that Saturday night. She accepted. *Why not?* She had quarreled with Don, and her brother and father would be at Serenity Farm visiting Gloria. "I think it will be fun. What shall I wear?"

"Something special," Kelton answered. "These people are a bit special themselves. The kids go to Choate and when they come home they invite some of the better locals to call."

Laura thought Kelton spent a lot of time worrying about prestige. She wondered if he'd been interested in Marilyn because she wore beautiful clothes and lived in a fancy house. But why was he interested in her?

She knew it was crazy to have broken up with Don over nothing and she didn't like Kelton very much. Still, it would be good to have some place to go this weekend. She felt miserable and she was even glad that Marilyn had been interested in Kelton. Perhaps it would even the score a bit if Laura dated him. In her heart, Laura knew that something was wrong with her thinking but she couldn't control it.

Even as she was studying with Kelton in the library, she was hoping Don would come in. It wasn't likely, but Laura was still wishing that the next time she saw Don he would greet her quietly and they would pick up the pieces.

They got a lot of studying done in an hour but Don didn't come in. When Kelton closed his English book, he said, "Your boyfriend Don is in my physics class."

"Ex-boyfriend."

"Good!" Kelton said. "And I bet I beat him on the test tomorrow too."

Waves of remorse attacked Laura. So that was it. Kelton was the other top student in Don's physics class. Kelton wanted whatever Don had — including her. She wanted to break the date right then and there but she didn't have the courage. She just stood up and said, "I'll see you Saturday. I have to get home."

Kelton smiled that charming smile of his and said, "Excuse me for not walking you home. I want to squeeze the time."

Don didn't call her that night and he didn't try to talk to her when he saw her at school. By Thursday, Laura understood that Don was really finished with her. She felt awful about it and she was sure Kelton wasn't her type, but she was glad he was so friendly. It was hard avoiding Don and Marilyn, so when Kelton walked her to classes she was grateful. She spent her lunch hours in the library and developed a technique of lingering long enough after class in one room to appear to be rushing to her next one. With these devices, she was able to avoid talking to anyone, even Marilyn.

She wanted to call Don on Thursday evening but she didn't. She was too angry that he'd taken her words so seriously. She was absolutely determined that she wasn't going to be the first one to speak. Surely if he cared for her, he would show it.

On Friday, she learned something that quashed the hope he would ever call again. A freshman girl said, "Hi, Laura. I hear you have a date with Kelton tomorrow."

Laura didn't even know the girl. She asked, "Where did you hear that?"

"Oh, everyone knows you dropped Don for Kelton. It's all over school."

Laura forced herself to keep smiling. "That's not what happened."

"Really? What did happen?"

Laura shook her head and smiled at the girl's eagerness for gossip. "Everything's complicated, you know." She picked up her comb and left the girl's room without putting on lipstick.

She gave her little brother the same answer that evening when he demanded, "Why won't you go see Gloria?"

But Tommy wasn't the sort to be put off with philosophical sayings. He asked her again at dinnertime. In a way, Laura was glad that Tommy wouldn't give up. He seemed to be the one person in her life who wasn't driven away by her moods.

She said, "I won't be going, but you will, Tommy Tiger. When you come home, you can tell me all about it."

Tommy nodded and added, "Is it all right if I tell Gloria you miss her too? Can I tell her you want her to come home?

Her father looked up from his newspaper and said sharply, "Tommy!"

But Laura was gentle with the boy in spite of her dad's obvious fears. She said, "You don't have to tell her anything. But if you want, you could tell her that I love her."

That much, at least, Laura knew was true. More than that, she just couldn't manage. The idea of having Gloria back still horrified her. But apparently, she was going to have some time to get used to the idea. When Tommy came in from his Saturday visit, he said, "Mama says she can't come home for a long time. She says she's been sick."

Laura was waiting for Kelton to pick her up and trying to appear absolutely indifferent to Tommy's glowing report of his mother.

"She sent her love, Laura. I told her you wanted to come but you couldn't. I told her you loved her a whole lot. But I didn't say you wanted her to live with us again." Tommy looked at his sister anxiously and asked, "Did I do right?"

Laura looked down at the little boy that she had cared for for so long. She felt as though her heart might break, he looked so small and vulnerable and desperate for love. She said, "Tommy Tiger, you did exactly right."

He sighed and nodded happily. "She did say she would go on the scout trip with me. She won't come to the house but she'd like to see the ships."

Laura shivered. *The White Rabbit is turning into the Snow Queen*, Laura thought. Again, it was as if she was frozen absolutely still. She could feel nothing, she could say nothing. Her head told her she was jealous, but her heart told her nothing. She patted Tommy on the head and said, "That's nice. Now here comes Kelton. When I introduce him, be sure and shake his hand."

"I like Don better," Tommy pronounced loyally, though he hadn't even seen this rival.

So do I, Laura thought. *So do I.*

CHAPTER 6

Though Tommy's loyalty to Don seemed childish, Laura wondered if her disloyalty wasn't worse. Within minutes, Kelton made it clear that his chief reason for taking Laura to the party was a part of his need to compete with Don. He gloated. "Beat your old boyfriend on a physics quiz yesterday."

"Good grades mean a lot to you, don't they."

Kelton shrugged. "It's a snap for me. Still, I do enjoy coming out on top of the class."

If he noticed that Laura was very silent on the trip to the party, he said nothing. *Perhaps he's glad*, Laura thought. Kelton was a non-stop talker and he told her a lot about the people they were going to visit. Some of it, she would rather not have known.

"Judge Wallace had to resign. They said he was involved in a shady business deal — a bribe or something. Anyway, I guess it didn't matter because he had loads of money. My mother and his oldest daughter went to school together in Virginia. It was one of those fancy finishing schools . . ."

Kelton sneaked a look out of the corner of his eye to see if Laura as impressed. Laura was amazed that anyone cared about things like that anymore. When she said nothing, Kelton went on, "They have this country home in Stockbridge. You'll see. They're only here for a few months out of the year. The rest of the time, they're in New York City or Palm Beach."

Kelton pulled the car into a circular driveway in front of a beautiful old stone farmhouse on a slight hill. "There," he pronounced, and leaned back to look at the house.

He sounds so proud of having wealthy friends, Laura thought. It's as though he's done something special. Out loud, she said, "It's a lovely house."

Kelton looked at her very carefully, reached out and adjusted the collar on her dress. He said, "You look fine."

If she hadn't had so many real problems of her own, Kelton's desperate snobbishness would have probably made her nervous. As it was, she was still half-thinking of her brother Tommy's report of his visit to Gloria. She was also thinking of Don.

The party was small and pleasant. She liked most of the guests and was particularly attracted to Judge Wallace, who cooked delicious steaks over a fireplace-barbecue in the huge old farm kitchen. She helped him with the serving and clean-up without thinking.

After supper, she took a paper towel and began wiping off the top of the serving table. Kelton came over and said in an angry voice, "Laura, the maid will do that."

Laura blushed and the Judge came to her defense. "Now, Kelton, you leave my assistant alone. We were getting along just fine without you." Though he spoke pleasantly, he obviously meant Kelton to take the admonition seriously.

It was Kelton's turn to blush and Laura looked gratefully at the Judge and said, "I guess I'm used to helping in the kitchen. I do all the cooking at home."

Judge Wallace nodded his head and said, "Never let anyone make you ashamed of being a worker, Laura. It's an honorable quality."

This time, Laura laughed. "All right. I'll remember that. You have a lovely home."

After supper, the Judge took Laura around the house and showed her his beautiful antiques and paintings. He was especially pleased when she admired some delicate porcelain figurines. "They were my mother's," Judge Wallace said. "You remind me of her."

Laura thought he might be kidding. She turned to look at him.

The Judge added, "You have the same serious sweetness she had. Grace is the old-fashioned word for that quality. You're a special young woman, Laura. Thank you for coming to my party."

In the next two weeks, Laura hung on to the Judge's praise to buoy her sagging spirits. At least one man had seen something special about her. As for herself, she felt lost without Don, though Kelton asked her out again and again. She went with him once to study in the library and have a Coke afterwards, and once to go to a movie. She was grateful for the distraction, but dating Kelton didn't do much to raise her flagging spirits.

At school, Don nodded pleasantly when she saw him but he didn't try to patch things up. After the break-up, she'd quit jogging for a week but felt so much worse that she started again. It wasn't much fun running alone but it was important to keep herself feeling healthy. She sometimes ran past Don and Marilyn, but usually she was able to spot Don's bright red hair far enough away to avoid them.

Since she had gym with Marilyn, there was no real way to avoid her. The Friday afternoon before the second race, Marilyn asked, "Will you come to a party at my place after the marathon?"

Laura shook her head quickly. "I feel funny around Don."

Marilyn made a face. "You and Don are so stubborn. You deserve each other."

Laura laughed and asked, "He says the same thing, huh?"

"I'd like to see you together again," Marilyn said. "You suit each other."

"You know, I always thought you were interested in Don for yourself," Laura admitted. "I think I've always been a little jealous."

Marilyn was quite serious. "You have nothing to be jealous of, you know. Don's still crazy about you. You're special."

Laura thought of a lot of things to say to Marilyn, but all she could really reply was, "I'll be at the party. I'll also come to the marathon."

Marilyn nodded happily. "Now that you know what a meddler I am, I'll tell you something else.

I don't know what's going to happen between you and Don, but I do know that Kelton is a real loser."

Laura grinned. "I didn't need anyone to tell me that. But thanks."

Laura hoped she and Don would find some way to get back together at Marilyn's party. She promised herself that no matter what happened, she wouldn't get upset. Either she'd talk to Don and he would be distantly polite, or she would talk to Don and he'd ask her out, or she'd talk to Don and. . . . *It doesn't matter what happens*, Laura told herself. *The important thing is I'm going to talk with Don.*

In a way, Laura was glad she was so nervous about seeing Don again because it kept her from dreading Gloria's first visit home quite as much. This was the big weekend, and though Laura had known it was coming for a month, every time she thought of actually confronting her mother for the first time in two years she froze.

Tommy and her father drove to Serenity Farm that Saturday right after lunch to pick Gloria up. Her father had really pushed to get Laura to make the two-hour drive with them, but she refused. Somehow, it seemed as though it was going to be easier to meet Gloria for the first time at home.

As Laura put the lunch dishes away, she looked around the kitchen at the shining tiles, the sparkling floors, and remembered the many, many hours she'd put in working in this room. Bitterness washed over her as she thought, *Her kitchen two years ago. My kitchen now. Whose kitchen tomorrow?*

Laura tossed the dishcloth on the rack and ran up the stairs to get ready for Marilyn's party. *You're crazy to worry about a kitchen*, she told herself. *You're only young once. Enjoy yourself.*

Laura dressed with care, brushing her long, golden hair back into soft waves behind her ears. She looked critically in the mirror and smiled tentatively at the young woman with the cool, green eyes. It was true. She did look like Gloria. Her mouth was a little fuller, her chin a bit rounder, but looking in the mirror was almost like looking at the past.

Laura moved restlessly from room to room, picking up objects and putting them down. The house was spotless and there was nothing to do now but wait. When she heard a car pull up and the car door slam, she took a deep breath and walked to the front door.

She stood in the doorway and watched her father and Gloria walk up the driveway to the house. As they came closer, Gloria opened her arms as if to embrace Laura.

Laura moved back quickly and said, "Hello, Gloria. Come in."

Gloria didn't hug her, but she did grab Laura's arm and held her still for a second as she said, "Let me look at you. Yes, you're beautiful. Your father was right."

Laura said nothing. Gloria looked heavier, tired, and older than she remembered, but she looked the same. It was a strange feeling to be looking into the clear green eyes of a mother she'd honestly never expected to see again.

The silence seemed long and painful — but her

father broke it by chattering about the drive. Gloria looked at Laura and winked. Laura knew the wink was intended to say, "Men!" She did not smile at her mother.

When Gloria let her go, Laura looked at her watch and said, "I'm on my way to a party. I'll be late."

Gloria looked bewildered. "A party?"

"Yes. It's the second track meet of a special co-ed competition. My friend Marilyn is running."

"But it's only two-thirty," Gloria said.

"I'm going to the end of the marathon first," Laura explained. "It started at twelve." She picked up her sweater and was gone before Gloria had a chance to say anything else.

She went to the finish line of the second marathon a half an hour before anyone was expected to finish. In a race of over twenty-six miles, most of these high school youngsters would take between four and five hours if they were able to complete the race at all. Waiting for Marilyn and Don was boring and depressing because there were very few others standing around.

Marilyn came in first among the women and Don placed second in the men. That gave them a co-ed place of first and Laura felt twinges of envy as she watched Marilyn accept the blue ribbon for her team. With a first and a third, Don and Marilyn had a good chance of winning the trip to Buffalo. Even though she'd just run twenty-six miles, Marilyn looked cool and beautiful as she came over to Laura. She said, "Thanks for coming out. Marathon races don't exactly draw a big crowd."

"Congratulations," Laura said. As Don came up, Laura's heart started beating with excitement.

He grinned at her and wiped his face off with a damp towel. "It's good to see you."

Marilyn added, "I'm glad you're already dressed. We'll go right to my house and get the stuff ready for the party. OK?"

Though Laura agreed quickly, Don said he had to go home first. He said, "I have to change and I have to put in a couple of hours on physics. See you around seven."

Marilyn pretended to be gravely disappointed. "The party starts at six. Don't forget, it's a picnic."

Don pointed to the sky. "I never heard of an April picnic in Massachusetts."

"It's a playroom picnic," Marilyn conceded. "But do hurry." She looked at Laura as though she expected her to chime in.

Laura said nothing. She felt awkward and silly standing beside these two runners. She wished she'd waited to dress for the party until later. Even though she was wearing white slacks and a sweater, she felt overdressed on a track field.

Don smiled briefly and trotted off toward his house. Tears of disappointment rose in Laura's eyes. She said, "Your ribbon is beautiful."

Marilyn said, "Don't be discouraged. Don really does work a lot."

Laura forced herself to laugh. "You don't have to explain Don to me. I've known him a long time. Now let's get going or the picnic won't be ready."

There was no real need to worry. By the time

she and Marilyn got to the Rogers house, Mrs. Rogers had everything just about finished.

Laura couldn't help comparing Marilyn's mother with Gloria. In a way, Laura supposed she was very lucky. At least Gloria had had enough problems of her own so that her kids had learned independence. Mrs. Rogers watched Marilyn's every move, warning her about salt shakers, reminding her of her promise to call a friend, and advising against the yellow sweater because it made Marilyn's skin seem sallow. If one could hover around a six-foot-tall teenager, then Mrs. Rogers hovered.

Marilyn seemed accustomed to her mother's nervousness and if she minded it, she didn't show it. For her own part, Laura tried to stay as far away from Mrs. Rogers as possible. Even so, at about fifteen minutes of six, as she was helping Mrs. Rogers put out little dishes of nuts, Mrs. Rogers said, "I understand your mother is coming home, dear."

Startled, Laura dropped a bag of peanuts on the floor. "Oh, I'm sorry!" she exclaimed, and dropped on her knees to try and catch them as they rolled around.

By the time the nuts were swept up, the first guest arrived and Laura was spared talking anymore to the prying Mrs. Rogers. She tried not to let it bother her that everyone seemed to know so much about her family, but she really hated it. She wondered how her mother felt coming back to Pittsfield. Laura doubted that Gloria would ever truly be accepted by people like Mrs. Rogers.

Soon the house was crowded with teenagers

who were eating hamburgers faster than she and Marilyn could cook them. It was almost eight o'clock when Don got there. The minute he walked into the room, Laura put down the plates she was stacking, took off her apron, and walked across the wide playroom floor. She was determined to try and patch things up with Don. She'd missed him a lot and just seeing him from across the room made her heart skip.

"Hi," she said. "Want to dance?"

"Sure." He led her over to the half of the playroom that served as a dance floor. For a while, they danced together without talking. Laura felt the music move through her body. It was good to be with Don and not have to explain anything.

The record stopped and a slow one began. Without saying anything at all, Laura opened her arms and Don stepped closer. Dreamily, Laura closed her eyes and sunk her head on Don's shoulder. *It's going to be all right*, Laura thought.

At that moment, she felt Don start, then stop. Before she opened her eyes, she knew it was Kelton's brash voice. "What are you doing with my girl?" he asked loudly.

Don stepped away. Laura called out, "Don, I'm not his girl. Don't go."

But Don turned from her and headed for the door. He looked white-faced and angry.

Laura wanted to follow him but she knew it wouldn't do any good. She practically hissed at Kelton, "Why did you do that? You know he's important to me!"

Kelton laughed loudly and said, "But, Laura, you're important to me."

Laura watched in despair as Don left the party without giving her a chance to explain. When Kelton tried to get her to dance, she pulled away from him and ran to the door. Don was gone and things were worse than ever between them.

She purposely avoided saying good-bye to Marilyn. Marilyn would be sympathetic and Laura couldn't afford to accept any sympathy from anyone. She felt too sorry for herself.

CHAPTER 7

When Laura woke on Sunday morning, her first thoughts were of the disastrous encounter with Don the night before. Why hadn't he waited long enough for her to explain? He'd been so unfair to run away like that.

It was after she smelled the bacon coming from the kitchen that she remembered Gloria was home. Quickly, Laura pulled on her jogging suit and brushed her hair. She felt so stiff and uncomfortable about having her mother in the house after two full years that she almost went out the front door without saying anything.

Tommy called to her so there was nothing to do but go into the kitchen. Tommy was beaming with happiness as he proudly announced, "Gloria fixed my breakfast. Pancakes and bacon too."

Laura smiled and said, "Smells good." She looked at her mother. "Hi, Gloria."

Her mother seemed to step forward, then stopped. She smiled tentatively and said, "You're so grown-up."

Laura smiled politely and nodded. "Sixteen, you know."

She turned to go through the door. Gloria asked, "Don't you want breakfast? Just the three of us?"

Laura ignored the pleading in her mother's question. She shook her head firmly and said, "I jog each morning for an hour. Then I'll have some of my own energy drink. No wasted calories."

Gloria's face seemed to crumple. She said softly, "I guess you're very healthy."

Laura nodded grimly. "I try." She didn't bother to tell her mother about the incipient ulcer, nor did she bother to explain that she jogged to relieve nervous tension. When she offered Gloria some of her special energy drink, Gloria laughed and said, "Nope. I'll stick to my carbohydrates for a while."

Laura turned to look critically at her mother. It was funny to see the ways in which Gloria had changed. She looked older than Laura remembered. In fact, Gloria looked quite a bit older, but more than that, her face seemed soft and hazy. Not the sharp beauty that she used to have. Of course, Gloria was fatter than she was the night she walked out two years ago.

Laura said, "You've put on weight."

Gloria blushed under the criticism. "I was very thin and they told me to eat. I guess I ate too much."

Laura felt sorry for her mother. It was a little like seeing a three-year-old apologize, but she could think of nothing nice to say. She asked, "Did you have trouble finding things in the kitchen?"

"Laura, are you going to treat me this way all day?"

"What way? I don't know what you mean."

Laura started pouring the milk and yeast into the blender.

"You treat me as though I were a stranger," Gloria said. She spoke softly, very timidly.

Laura raised her voice. "I can't hear you." She really had heard her mother, but it was as if some other crueler Laura was trying deliberately to make her mother miserable.

And Gloria was miserable — that was clear. Tears played around the edges of her eyes. She was silently pleading with Laura to take her in her arms — to tell her it was all right. *She wants me to be her mother*, Laura thought. Well, all right. If she wanted to act like a baby, that was her business. She — Laura — was grown-up now. She didn't have to be nice to anyone she didn't want to.

Laura asked, "Are you tired? Shall I wash the dishes?"

Gloria said in a muffled voice, "No, thanks."

Laura raised her voice again. "Let me put them away. I know where they go."

Gloria's face was crumpling again. Her voice was strained as she answered, "I know where they go too."

"No, you don't," Laura said sharply. "You haven't been here in two years. Go see Tommy."

Gloria dropped a glass and ran crying from the room. Laura felt guilty and awful, but at the same time there was a small smile playing around the edges of her mouth. She thought, *I'm turning into a terrible person.* Then, irrationally, she thought, *But it's all Gloria's fault.*

Laura was wiping the counter top when her father came in the kitchen, looking grim. He stood for a minute in the doorway, waiting for Laura to say something. When she ignored him, he asked, "How long do you intend to keep this up?"

"I don't know what you mean."

"Your mother is crying. You've managed to make her feel unwelcome very quickly."

Laura turned to face him. "All I did was offer to put away the dishes. I was trying to be nice."

"She said you ran her out of the kitchen."

Laura shrugged. "I offered to put away the dishes and she dropped a glass and ran out. I finished the dishes, picked up the glass, and now the kitchen is all hers." Laura hung the towel on the rack.

"Go up and apologize to your mother," her father demanded. "She wants to go back to Serenity Farm."

"What shall I apologize for?" Laura asked. "You want me to apologize for putting away the dishes? For picking up the broken glass? What do you want?" She knew her own voice was breaking into unreasonable shrillness, but she felt she had to defend herself.

"Let her alone," Gloria said as she appeared in the doorway. "I've explained to Tommy that I'm going early because I have a headache."

Gloria looked awful. Tears were running down her face and her eye makeup was running in dark black streaks. She spoke quietly, as though she were a very old and tired woman. "I knew it was going to be tough and it is. I'll be back but I need to get to the farm now."

"Stay," Laura offered. "If you want, I'll go out for the rest of the day."

Gloria looked at her with such sadness that Laura thought her heart might break. She wanted to run over and comfort her mother as she would Tommy. She did not. If Gloria was going to come back into their lives, she would have to understand that Laura couldn't go back to being a little girl just because her mother wanted it. Laura held her ground and watched impassively as Gloria shook her head.

"No, that won't work, We have to learn to work together again." When she saw Laura stiffen, Gloria laughed softly. "But not today. I understand that you're angry with me, Laura. Someday I hope to begin to make amends. Today I have to leave. I'm sorry." Gloria choked on those last words and ran from the room.

Laura poured herself a glass of milk and sat down at the kitchen table to leaf through the Sunday paper. The car was out of the driveway before she realized they'd taken Tommy with them. That meant there was no one to cook for. That meant she had the whole day alone with nothing to do. Since Gloria had come back into their lives, Laura had spent her Sundays alone.

Laura went up to her room to start work and discovered she was whistling. Quickly, she buried the feelings of triumph she felt about her mother's retreat. She didn't want to be the sort of person who gloated over someone else's weaknesses. Or was she already that sort?

CHAPTER 8

If Laura enjoyed the small triumph over her mother, she didn't enjoy the conversation with her father that evening. He was sharp and direct as he said, "Now here it is, Laura. Next Saturday, you are going to Serenity Farm with Tommy and me. You will be courteous to your mother if you cannot be loving. You will not shame her in front of her friends and you will do everything you can to keep from upsetting Tommy, your mother, or me."

"Don't I count?" Laura asked.

"You count but you're not going to destroy this family."

Laura stared at her father. "I'm not the one who destroyed the family. Gloria is."

Her father shook his head. "We live in the present, not the past. A day at a time, that's the rule from now on. Get it?"

Laura nodded her head. Ever since her father had started seeing Gloria again, he'd been repeating Alcoholics Anonymous slogans, such as "One day at a time" and "Easy does it."

Her father patted her shoulder. "You're a good girl, Laura. Once you gain some trust again, you'll be able to love your mother without fear. In the meantime, I ask you — no, I tell you — not to mess things up for all of us."

Laura cried herself to sleep that night and try as she would, she could not break her mood on Monday. Going back to school and facing Don's rejection made her home problems all the more difficult. He no longer spoke to her at all and she only saw him from a distance. She didn't pass him in the halls once that whole week, and when the next Saturday morning came and she got into the car to go to Serenity Farm with Tommy and her father, she felt almost as gloomy as she had a week earlier.

If her father noticed her mood, he ignored it. When he offered to let her drive, she knew he was trying to be nice. Though she'd gotten her license on her sixteenth birthday, she was seldom allowed to use the car. She forced herself to tease him, to cover her miserable mood. "You'd actually trust me?"

He made a face. "Well, if you don't want to . . ."

"I want to. Move over."

Laura slipped behind the wheel and turned the Oldsmobile onto the city street. Driving the car did cheer her up. She loved the feeling of power and control, loved driving through the gorgeous countryside. Though the day was cool, the trees were beginning to leaf out, and there was bright yellow forsythia all over the country landscape. "Another week and it will be flowering tree time," her father mused.

Laura nodded and didn't answer. She wanted to concentrate on her driving, to concentrate on the good feelings she got by maneuvering this powerful machine down country roads. *Life could be good if you were in control*, she thought. She resolved to be perfectly in control when she saw Gloria this time.

Gloria had obviously made the same resolution because she greeted Laura with a cool, composed smile and then turned all her attention to Tommy, who began a long recitation of the week's events. Laura watched her mother and brother laughing and talking together, and for the first time noticed that they smiled exactly alike. It was funny that she'd never noticed before how much Tommy looked like his mother. No one ever mentioned it — probably because she and Gloria looked so very much alike.

They were all sitting in wonderful old wicker rockers on the porch of Serenity Farm. Laura watched Tommy's face grow more and more animated as he told his mother a long, complicated story about his best friend's rabbit and the rules for their clubhouse. *I envy Tommy*, Laura thought. *He's so young. Young enough to forget.* Abruptly, she jumped out of the rocker and asked, "Is it all right if I go for a walk?"

Gloria nodded. "Head over to the falls. It's a lovely walk."

Laura started to ask Tommy if he wanted to come with her but decided against it. He looked so happy, she was sure he would refuse. She walked away from the treatment center and through a long, green meadow toward the distant foothills.

When she was about one half block away, she stopped and looked back at the beautiful farmhouse that was the original building for Serenity Farm. Funny how much the place was exactly as she'd imagined. It was a huge, old, white frame building, resting on top of a hill. Smaller buildings, where the guests and staff lived, surrounded the main house. They ate their meals, and held their meetings, and attended counseling sessions in the big house. In their spare time, they worked in the gardens or sat on the porch and looked out at the Massachusetts countryside.

It was serene here, Laura decided. In a way it was good to see Gloria in the place where she was living. Compared to the rest of the patients, she looked young and happy. And here, Gloria seemed softer and less tense. She'd been happy and relaxed as she talked of the others. Over and over, she'd repeated her gratitude. "I have so much left," she'd said and hugged her son close to her.

My mother is happy, Laura thought. Somehow, Gloria's happiness only made Laura more miserable. She turned from Serenity Farm and plodded through the newly grown weeds.

She didn't know exactly where she was going, and it was cool — so cool that she pulled her sweater around her tightly, then broke into a light jog. The running always helped. There was something about the exercise and the discipline that took her mind off her problems. When a small brown rabbit ran across her path, she laughed aloud. *There's the White Rabbit's cousin.*

Now she could hear running water and she decided she must be close to the falls her mother had mentioned. She turned onto a worn path and followed it down to the edge of the land. Then she could see a slight slope, and beyond that a lovely, fast-running brook and a medium-sized stream.

Laura hesitated by the path, trying to decide whether to go down the path to the footbridge or not. It was beautiful and she wanted to get closer, but there was a young woman down there already. She was wearing a red and orange striped tee shirt and was sitting on a rock, holding her face to the sun.

Laura didn't want to disturb her and so she turned to go. "Come on down," the young woman called, and waved to Laura.

The young woman looked as if she were about Laura's age. Her long brown hair was tied with a piece of bright yellow yarn. She said. "I'm Jerri Hill. You're Gloria's daughter, aren't you?"

Laura stood hesitantly at the foot of the small boulder where Jerri sat. She didn't really want to get into any conversations with teenagers. Still, courtesy was as natural to Laura as brushing her teeth. She said, "I'm Laura Manning. I'm visiting my mother today. Who are you visiting?"

Jerri laughed. "I'm a resident. I've been here six months this week."

Laura was amazed that anyone Jerri's age could be an alcoholic. She asked, "How old are you?"

"Nineteen," Jerri answered. "I know I look younger. But I was nineteen two weeks ago."

"Nineteen is so young," Laura said.

Jerri nodded briskly. "Very young to be a drunk, but think of the wonderful life I have ahead of me now that I know how to live."

Laura grinned and finished for her. ". . . Live one day at a time."

Jerri nodded. "I guess you've been hearing the same slogans, haven't you? Well, they all work. I was in real trouble when I got here six months ago. I'd been on the streets for almost four years. I was malnourished, suicidal, and addicted to alcohol and pills. Now look at me. I'm alive and on my way to a new life next week."

"You're leaving Serenity Farm?"

"I was praying for courage when you came up. Going back to Albany on Wednesday. It's a little scary."

"Back to your folks?" Laura usually didn't ask personal questions, but Jerri was so open that she felt comfortable with her.

Jerri shook her head. "My folks are divorced. I don't know where my father is and my mother has problems of her own."

"I'm sorry."

Jerri shook her shoulders and seemed to be making a conscious decision to shake herself out of her depression. "I'm sorry too. But I already have a job and I'll be sharing an apartment with some A.A. friends." She laughed and interrupted herself. "I'm speaking at the meeting tonight, so you'll hear my story. Let's talk about you. How are you doing?"

"I'm all right," Laura answered. She couldn't tell this young woman about her problems. What would a person who had been through what Jerri Hill had been through think of a small matter like losing a boyfriend or not wanting your mother back home?

"Gloria coming back was quite a shock, wasn't it?" Jerri asked softly. "I think I'd be very angry if my mother showed up two years later and tried to be my mother again."

Laura asked, "Does my mother talk about me?" The thought was almost too much to bear.

"We share our problems with each other. Gloria loves you so much, but she doesn't know what to say or do to reach you. I'm near your age and I've been trying to help her realize that you're grown. She'll never recover the years she lost. It's very sad for her."

Laura bent over and picked up a flat rock. She skimmed it onto the stream. "I know I'm supposed to feel sorry for my mother. I hear all that stuff about alcoholism being a disease and I know she can't help herself. But I can't be nice to her. All I can think of when I see her is how she left us. All I can think of when I see her is now she's come back and she's trying to take over again. She's trying, I suppose, but . . ."

". . . But you need time to accept her. You're a nice person, Laura. Don't let your resentment about the past spoil the present."

"Why do people drink?" Laura asked. For one minute, she felt ashamed of the question but it had been on her mind since she was in the fifth grade and first understood that her mother was a drunk. At last, she had been able to ask it of a real alcoholic. She waited patiently as Jerri seemed to search for an answer.

"No one knows why some people drink normally and others drink alcoholically. Some people think alcoholics are troubled people with psychological problems. Other people think there is something about the alcoholic's body chemistry that makes it impossible for him to drink like others. No one really knows, Laura."

Laura nodded quietly. It was the same old answer. No one knew why. This young woman could tell her nothing more than her parents.

Jerri looked at her watch. "It's suppertime. When we get back to the farm, I'll give you my phone number and address for my new apartment. You might want to call me."

"I don't get to Albany much."

Jerri laughed and chided, "Never turn down an offer of friendship. Who knows when we might need a friend?"

When they got back to the farm, Laura asked Jerri to eat with them. It made suppertime much easier. With Jerri by her side, she was able to watch Tommy and Gloria and her father chatting and laughing together without the great stab of jealousy she usually experienced. *That's what it is,* she told herself. *It's jealousy.*

By the time dinner was over, her efforts must have shown because Gloria put her hand on Laura's head and asked, "Are you all right?"

Laura drew back quickly. Gloria's touching her brought back a lot of childhood memories. She wanted to get as far away from those old feelings as possible. She managed to say, "I'm fine. Just tired."

Gloria apparently realized that she had overstepped her limits and her face crumpled into the familiar apologetic look. Laura immediately felt guilty, and at the same time she wanted to shout at her mother, "Go away! Go away!" She did nothing except excuse herself from the table.

When she got back, Gloria and Jerri were in heavy conversation and Laura was sure it was about her. She hated the knowledge that they shared secrets. What right had her mother to discuss family problems with strangers?

Laura didn't want to go to the A.A. meeting after dinner but there was no way to get out of it. Somehow, the thought of a roomful of people with alcohol problems was too depressing to face. She knew that Serenity Farm had open meetings on Saturday night and invited speakers from all over. Though she had never been to an A.A. meeting, her father had gone to several open ones and had tried to tell her about them.

Laura made one attempt to avoid the meeting by saying, "I think I'll watch television with Tommy in the lobby."

Her father answered briefly, "No. You'll come with your mother and me."

Laura followed meekly into the large meeting room with folding chairs. Gloria said, "I'm going to sit in that section with the other residents. You two better find seats up front."

Laura was glad to sit unobtrusively and watch the others mill about, getting coffee, talking a mile a minute, and laughing loudly. She was amazed at how happy everyone seemed. There was a lot of laughter, and to Laura much of it seemed too loud to be real. Still, there were about two hundred people in the room and most of them were alcoholics. Most of them looked prosperous, happy, and contented. None of them were drinking.

According to her mother, most of the people here tonight were graduates of Serenity Farm who came back out of loyalty and gratitude, either to speak or visit with others or the staff. Laura had to admit that Alcoholics Anonymous worked for them.

At exactly eight o'clock, a man opened the meeting by reading the Alcoholics Anonymous preamble, and then he said, "Our first speaker is Jerri H. from Albany." He sat down and Jerri walked toward the speaker's stand. Laura could tell that she was nervous by the way she held on to the side of the podium and cleared her throat.

"My name is Jerri," she began. "And I am an alcoholic." Jerri told how she began drinking at the age of thirteen and used alcohol to avoid her problems in school and with her parents. As she talked, Laura found herself listening carefully to Jerri's story. Tears came to her eyes as Jerri talked of the growing dependence of a lonely teenage girl on alcohol. When Jerri told of her suicide attempts, Laura gripped the side of her chair. How horrible it must have been.

Then Jerri began to talk about coming to Alcoholics Anonymous and being admitted to the treatment center. She spoke for about twenty-five minutes and then sat down. She walked directly over to Laura as the chairman announced a coffee break. Laura squeezed her hand and said, "You were wonderful."

During the break, Jerri wrote her address and phone number on a piece of paper and handed it to Laura. She said, "Stick it in your wallet, Laura, and call me anytime. Day or night. I want to be your friend."

As Jerri watched, Laura tucked the paper behind her driver's license in her wallet and said, "I'll try to visit you sometime soon."

Before Jerri could reply, the chairman introduced the next speaker. He said, "This is John W. from Stockbridge."

Laura almost fell off her chair as Judge Wallace walked to the speaker's podium. She whispered to Jerri, "I met him once. He's a judge."

Jerri smiled. "Yes, we get all kinds. Politicians, bank presidents, judges, and juvenile delinquents."

The Judge began his talk by thanking Jerri for her excellent message. Unlike that young woman, he wasn't nervous at all. As he spoke, Laura forgot that the man was telling a tragic tale of loss. By the end of thirty minutes, Laura had laughed so much she was crying. Yet, she knew that she had been moved by his story as well.

Of course he got it all back, Laura thought. *No wonder he's so cheerful*. It was then that Laura understood that her own mother expected to get everything back too. Laura felt that cold anger close in on her again. What right had her mother to get off scot-free?

She left the meeting immediately and went directly to the car, without even saying good-night to Jerri or hello to the Judge. She'd heard as much as she wanted to hear.

Though Laura found herself thinking about the A.A. meeting a lot the next week, she refused to go back the next Saturday, claiming too much homework. Her father didn't argue with her much. He just said. "You're sixteen, Laura. I guess you have to make your own mistakes."

Laura spent Saturday afternoon cleaning closets and cupboards. The time when Gloria would be returning to live permanently with the family was coming closer, and she had developed a real need to have the house absolutely immaculate. Laura knew it was silly — that Gloria had never been that fussy a housekeeper and that she was in no position to criticize, yet she scrubbed all weekend.

The harder she worked, the more miserable she became. Tommy and her father were absolutely glowing with the knowledge that her mother would be returning soon. Though they tried to be nice to her, Laura knew they were unappreciative of the work she was doing. It seemed to Laura that every other word out of Tommy's mouth was about his mother.

School was worse than home. Though she still managed to spend her lunch hours in the library, and though she was getting nearly straight A's because she spent so much extra time studying, she practically spoke to no one.

Marilyn was still friendly and she offered bits of news each day when they saw each other in gym. She often invited her over to study, but Laura always turned down the invitations. They didn't talk about Don at all anymore because there wasn't anything to say. More than once, she picked up the phone to call Don but she always put it down again. Laura missed him very much, but she couldn't get over the feeling that he would call her if he really missed her.

It was getting harder and harder to get out of bed in the morning. By the first of May, she'd almost given up jogging. Not eating a real lunch was bothering her stomach. In fact, she was so depressed that the pain in her stomach was worse than ever. The Wednesday before her mother's next visit home, Laura went to the doctor.

Doctor Thomas prescribed what he called a non-addictive muscle relaxant and asked, "What do you think your father would think if I sent you to a psychiatrist?"

Laura choked out, "I'm not crazy."

"No, you're not. But you're depressed and you've got a pretty troublesome symptom there. It might be a good idea."

Laura shook her head. "The pills will help."

The doctor sighed and patted her arm. "Laura, you're trying too hard. You're practically a child."

"I'm sixteen," Laura protested. All the time, her mind was racing with the words, *He thinks I'm crazy. He thinks I'm crazy.*

Doctor Thomas didn't argue. He just said, "Understand your mother's coming home soon. Maybe that will help."

Laura thought about telling Doctor Thomas that it was her mother's return which was making her feel so sick, but she didn't. She just took the pills from him and went home quickly so she could get dinner ready for Tommy and her father.

When her father came in from work, he asked, "What did the doctor say?"

"He gave me some pills." She popped the top off some orange juice and added a bit to the sauce she was making for the baked chicken. Her hand was shaking. *Maybe I am crazy*, she thought.

Her father didn't pursue the subject. "Smells good in here. You've been a wonderful help to us, Laura. We'll never be able to pay you back."

She shook her head, at least partly to hold back the tears that filled her eyes. She said, "There's nothing to pay back. Do you want rice?"

"Your mother is coming home Saturday to spend the weekend. I hope things go better."

"They will."

"No. I mean I hope they really go better. This breach in the family has got to be healed."

Laura put the orange juice on the top of the cabinet. She spoke slowly and carefully, as though she might break something if she wasn't careful. She said, "Dad, I'm glad you and Gloria are back together. I'm glad for Tommy and I'm glad that Gloria is getting well. It's just that when I'm around her, I have the feeling that she's trying too hard. I know what she wants and I can't give it to her — not yet."

"She wants your love. That's natural."

"She wants me to give her back her past. She wants me to say everything is all right. She wants me to change into the fourteen-year-old kid she left behind. She wants to come into my life and be the mother she never was. She should be able to understand that it's too late."

Her father nodded his head. "Some of that is true, Laura. In many ways you're older than Gloria. You can understand things better than she does. You can help us if you try. Laura, I'd hate to lose her again. I love her so much."

Laura could think of nothing else to say and her father didn't pursue the conversation. During supper, they listened to Tommy's chatter. When dinner was over, she went into the living room and picked up the telephone.

She wanted to call Don but instead she called Kelton. When he answered, she asked, "Hi, want to go to the movies Saturday night? My treat."

Kelton was delighted and insisted that he would take her out for pizza before the movie. Laura hung up the telephone with mixed feelings. In her heart, she knew Kelton was not a good person for her to date, yet he was available and interested. At least dating Kelton would get her out of the house for a part of Saturday afternoon and evening. She could also claim homework and stay in her room most of the rest of the time.

Her father wanted her to help keep Gloria. Fair enough. If she couldn't do anything else, she would stay out of the way. What more could they ask?

CHAPTER 9

Laura came in from jogging on Saturday morning just as Tommy and Gloria were cooking pancakes. They were laughing and talking together so cheerfully that Laura felt happy for her younger brother. For one moment, her heart melted and she thought, *Whatever makes Tommy happy*. She said, "Hi, Gloria. You look good."

Gloria smiled hopefully. Her eyes were shining as she returned the greeting.

Laura pushed her hair out of her eyes. "I'm bushed," she said. "I ran ten miles this morning before you got here. Now it's homework time."

"Your father told me how you lost out on the track team. I hope we can make it up to you someday."

The old resentment stirred in Laura. How did her mother hope to make it up to her? Didn't she realize that time doesn't move backwards? Laura poured her breakfast drink out of the blender and said, "It wasn't important. Anyway, now that Tommy spends so much time with you, I'm making straight A's in school."

Gloria beamed approval. "I remember how much you wanted to go to Miss Merriweather's when you were younger. I'm so glad that your education at Central High is turning out well."

"I'd almost forgotten Miss Merriweather's," Laura said. She gulped the remainder of her energy drink and headed for the door.

"Tommy and I are going to the lake this afternoon. Want to come along?" Gloria asked.

"Can't. Have to study."

"You could bring your books. It will be fun," Gloria urged.

"Mama says it's too cold to swim," Tommy added. "I'm going to fish."

Laura headed for the door. "Sorry. Not this time." She went up to her room and closed the door quickly. She was already sorry she'd stopped to talk to her mother in that way. All it did was make her feel bad when her mother started talking to her as though she was twelve years old. Laura's stomach began to hurt and she bent over with pain. She would have to take one of the pills the doctor gave her.

As she went to the bathroom to get water, she thought about what Doctor Thomas had said. He'd said she was anxious — too anxious for a teenager.

Laura swallowed the pill, made a face at herself in the mirror, and whispered, "Stop feeling sorry for yourself. Hit the books. You've got a date tonight."

Somehow, the thought of a date with Kelton didn't cheer her up much. She missed Don so much. Laura had almost given up the hope of getting back together with him. *He doesn't care about me.* Laura shook her head at the reflection in the mirror and went back to her room.

For the next four hours, she read history books for her special project. She was so engrossed in her work that she didn't hear the knock on the door. Gloria was standing inside the room when she spoke. "Laura, I want to talk with you."

Laura was so startled she jumped. "What do you want?"

Gloria sat down in the chair beside Laura's desk without being asked. "There's an Alateen meeting at St. Michael's Church this evening. It's for the children of alcoholics. There will be other kids with your problem there. I'd like you to go."

"I have a date."

"You have a date with a boy you don't like. You made the date so you could avoid me. You're making your life miserable to punish me. I want you to go to this meeting tonight, Laura. It will help you."

"How do you know I don't like him?" Laura asked incredulously.

"I know you, Laura. I'm your mother."

"Gloria, I'm trying to be polite. I'm doing my best to keep the family happy. But don't push me. Please don't push."

"I have a right to push a little," Gloria said firmly. "I'm your mother."

Laura noticed that her mother's mouth was trembling and her hands were clasped firmly in her lap. *She's afraid*, Laura thought. *She's got this whole speech rehearsed and she's afraid.* She said, "Gloria, you'll have to excuse me. I have work."

"Don't dismiss me!" Gloria's voice was shrill.

Laura turned her back and bent over her history book. Gloria grabbed Laura's shoulder and pulled her around. Laura was surprised that her mother's hands were so strong. Laura turned back, crossed her arms, and said, "All right. You've obviously got the whole thing rehearsed. Say your speech." Gloria's voice was trembling but it sounded stronger than Laura had heard it since she'd come back. "You're right. I *do* have some things to say. I *have* rehearsed them. I lie awake nights thinking of ways to make you understand. I see your cold face . . . your unforgiving eyes . . ." Gloria crumpled and buried her face in her hands.

Laura handed her a tissue and said, "I'm not the one who has to forgive you. There's nothing to forgive."

Gloria blew her nose, wiped her eyes, and continued. "I *want* your forgiveness but I know that will take time. It's you I want to talk about. It's *you* I'm concerned about. I know you're unhappy. I hate to see you being so self-destructive. I want to help you, Laura. Laura, tell that awful boy you can't go out and go to the Alateen meeting. It will help you."

"I don't need help."

Gloria stood up. "All right, then do it for Tommy. Don't you think he knows how unhappy you are? Do it for your father. He worries about you all the time. Laura, I don't want to come back home if it means that you're going to be miserable."

"I'm not miserable. I'm just busy." Laura hated

herself as the cold, crisp words tumbled from her mouth.

Gloria drew back as though slapped. She said, "All right. At least I tried and I haven't given up. As for your attitude toward me, don't think I intend to let you make me as miserable as you're making yourself."

Gloria gulped for air, and then continued. "I intend to be happy and you can be happy too. It's true I can't mend the past, but I'm living my life as best I can now. You're angry and I understand that but I have a right to recovery. I'm an alcoholic but as long as I don't drink I can live a fairly normal life. I have a right to a decent life, Laura. I've paid my dues."

Laura looked up from her history book long enough to ask, "Don't you think you're being a little dramatic?"

CHAPTER 10

When Kelton Kott came to pick up Laura, her mother answered the door. She called to Laura who made the introductions smoothly. Her mother behaved as though there was nothing wrong between them. She seemed just like the old Gloria as she kissed Laura lightly on the cheek and said, "Have a good time. Not too late, Laurie."

"Don't wait up," Laura said. Funny how comfortable it felt to have her mother standing in that doorway. Laura was a little ashamed about feeling so good that Gloria was as nice and pretty as she was. Kelton always made her feel as though he was inspecting her.

As they pulled out the drive, Kelton said, "Your mother is nice."

Laura chose to ignore the tinge of surprise in his voice. "I'm glad we're going for pizza. I love pizza."

"Yes," Kelton said. "You and Don went there a lot, didn't you?"

"I think the only reason you date me is to make Don jealous," Laura accused.

She knew she'd hit a sore spot when Kelton blushed slightly. She asked, "Don beating you in physics again?"

"Certainly not!" Kelton bristled.

By the time they got to the pizza parlor, she was sorry she'd asked Kelton out. What was it her mother had called her? Self-destructive. Was it self-destructive to want to go out once in a while? What was she supposed to do?

"You're not listening," Kelton accused.

"Sorry," Laura said. "I was thinking about my grades. There's a good chance I'll take top honors this year."

"You?" Kelton asked.

"Yes, me. Now let's hurry or we'll be late for the movie." She stood up and put her sweater around her shoulders. Kelton followed her to the door. When they got to the car, he stepped in front of her and said, "Let me open the door, Laura."

"OK." She waited patiently while he held the door for her. Once inside the car, Kelton said, "I like to be a gentleman. You should let me open doors for you. I like . . ."

"Don't tell me what I should do, Kelton. Let's just hurry or the movie will start." Laura knew her impatience with Kelton showed but she didn't care. This was absolutely the last time she was going out with him. She didn't like him and that was that.

Kelton was obviously hurt. They didn't talk until intermission when Kelton asked gruffly if she wanted some popcorn. She shook her head no and he went out to get some for himself. She felt vaguely uncomfortable, but there was nothing to do but get through the evening. If she went home this early, she'd have to admit that her mother was right. Besides, it would require a lot of energy to talk Kelton into taking her home. After all, the movies had been her idea, not his. Laura's stomach grumbled and she took one of the pills for indigestion that the doctor gave her. She shouldn't have eaten that pizza, though.

Kelton came back with two boxes of popcorn and a big grin on his face. He said, "We're invited to a party after the movie. I said we'd go."

"Oh, Kelton, I have to go right home."

"No you don't," Kelton reminded her complacently. "You told your mother not to wait up."

Laura decided she needed more than the indigestion pill. She looked at her watch. It was too early for another of the muscle relaxants. Still, it would be nice. She opened her purse, then snapped it closed again. Was that how her mother got hooked on alcohol? Always looking for something to ease the pain? Laura hated having to take the pills at all. She certainly wasn't going to take them except *exactly* the way the doctor ordered.

Much to her surprise, the movie was so good that Laura was able to forget her date, forget her fight with her mother, even forget her stomach ache for a while. She laughed and laughed at one spot. It felt good to be laughing again. As she wiped the tears from her eyes, she thought, *What's happened to me? I used to laugh all the time.*

She went over the changes in her life during the last few months. It seemed as though everything was crumbling at once. Was her mother right? Was it possible that all she had to do was change her attitude?

Right then and there, she decided she would try to be happy again. She could work on that a little bit at a time. Maybe she was truly making herself miserable. Well, she could stop that. She was young, attractive, bright, and had everything in the world to be happy about.

When the lights went on, she turned to Kelton and said, "I love Woody Allen."

"Apparently," Kelton said.

Laura was determined not to let him destroy her evening. She said, "He's just wonderful. Now, where's the party?"

"Oh, that's a surprise," Kelton said smoothly as he maneuvered the car out of the parking space. "I ran into some kids at the popcorn stand and they invited us."

Laura decided it was probably the Smithers twins from Judge Wallace's family. No one else would make him look that self-satisfied.

When they pulled up in front of Tommy Burns's house, Laura turned to Kelton and said, "You might have told me." Tommy was a good friend of Don's so there was a chance he'd be there.

"I wanted to surprise you."

Laura shook her head but said nothing as she glanced anxiously in the car mirror to see if she looked all right. She was wearing a new coral summer blouse even though the night was cool. She knew Kelton wanted to make Don jealous but there wasn't much she could do about that. Besides, she'd just made a resolution to be happy, no matter what.

The party was in full swing when they got there. Marilyn was standing by a Ping-Pong table covered with food. She called, "Hey, Laura, over here."

Laura walked straight toward Marilyn, leaving Kelton to fend for himself. If he had to show her off, that was his problem. She'd decided she wasn't going to let Kelton Kott, her mother, Donald Douglas, or anyone else keep her from having a good time. She said, "Hi, Marilyn. Good to see you."

Marilyn nodded happily. "The food's great. Why didn't you tell me you were coming? We could have come together."

"I'm with Kelton."

Marilyn's face changed slightly, then she shrugged and said, "What's a girl to do on Saturday night."

"Uh huh," Laura agreed. "But you're braver. You came alone?"

Marilyn nodded. "Don and I ran this morning. I asked him to go with me — nothing serious you understand — but he had to study for physics."

"Too bad for Kelton. I'm sure he brought me just to make Don jealous. Not that Don cares."

Marilyn popped a spoonful of mustard on her hot dog. "He cares. In fact, he asked if you would be here."

Laura felt the blood rush to her head. Suddenly, she wasn't pretending to be happy anymore. She really was. She asked, "Are you sure?"

"Sure I'm sure. I keep trying to tell you two that you're being very foolish. Gather ye rosebuds while ye may . . . You're only young once . . .

Here, want this?" Marilyn held out a hot dog covered with mustard, relish, onions, and catsup.

Laura laughed aloud and said, "Just the thing for my temperamental tummy. I'll fix my own, thanks." She put a hot dog on a bun and added a little catsup. Then she asked, "I don't suppose they'd be serving milk?"

It was Marilyn's turn to laugh. "Not unless it comes in pop-top cans. There might be some in the kitchen, though."

Laura took a bottle of 7-up from the bucket at the end of the table. "I'll do fine with this."

Marilyn asked, "How's your mom?"

Laura was in such a good mood, she didn't mind the question. She bit into the hot dog and answered, "My mom is just fine. Looks younger every day and seems very happy. She and Dad are like lovebirds. Tommy is ecstatic."

"And Laura?"

"Laura's got more time than she's had in years. I don't have Tommy underfoot anymore. Gloria always cooks on weekends. I'm almost ready to take up jigsaw puzzles or something."

Her voice must have sounded authentically happy because Marilyn said warmly, "I'm so glad for you, Laura. It's kind of like a story or something. I mean, your mother coming home after all this time."

"Yes, it is." She was determined to keep her cheerful mood. Looking around the room, she said, "Let's see who I can ask to dance."

"How about Kelton?" Marilyn teased.

"Why not?" Laura agreed. She headed across the den floor to ask him but as she crossed the room, Don appeared in the doorway. She stopped in the middle of the floor, wavered for just a second, and changed her course. She went up to Don and said, "Hi, I was hoping you'd be here."

"Want to dance?" Don asked.

Laura nodded, then her smile faded. She said, "I forgot. I'm with Kelton. In fact, I think he brought me just so you'd feel bad."

Don grinned and held out his arms. "Worked once but it won't work a second time. Even dummies can learn."

Laura sighed and looked at Don with happy eyes. She said, "Don, I want you to know I really miss you."

He held her tightly as they moved around the floor. He said slowly, carefully, "I've wanted to explain something. I miss you too, Laurie. More than you probably think."

Laura snuggled happily against his shoulder. Don kept right on talking. "I want to explain. It's hard for me but it is important. The thing is, I can't stand fights. I never talk about it but you should know. My folks fought all the time when I was young. I hated it. I promised myself I'd never get into one of those off-again, on-again romances."

Laura laughed lightly and kissed Don on the cheek. "All right, Don. Let's just make it an on-again romance."

He nodded gravely.

Laura traced her finger along the edge of Don's ear. "Good old Don. Always serious, always steady. I'm glad we're together again."

Don nodded. He said, "I'll call you Sunday

night when I get home from Springfield. We'll run together on Monday morning?"

"Aren't you taking me home?" Laura asked in dismay.

Don shook his head. "No, Laura. You came with Kelton. It wouldn't be right."

"But Kelton doesn't care about me. He just wants to make you feel bad. Why do you care about him?"

Don shook his head stubbornly. "You came with Kelton."

Laura shook her head. "Don, Don, you're so . . ." Then she burst out laughing with happiness. "You're so *Don*. And I did miss you."

It wasn't long before Kelton came over and said he wanted to go home. Laura agreed meekly and said good-bye to everyone. When she came to Marilyn and Don, she grinned and said, "Dance one for me. Cinderella just turned into a pumpkin."

Marilyn made a face and said, "There's a lesson somewhere in all this."

Laura laughed again and turned from them. She smiled at Kelton and said, "OK, Prince Charming, let's go."

Kelton was not amused. He held her arm as they went to the door. On the porch, he demanded, "Have you been drinking?"

"Drinking? Of course not."

"You seem awfully happy all of a sudden," Kelton said. He was obviously very annoyed.

Laura sat very still all the way home. She knew Kelton was angry with her for having such a good time and because she'd made up with Don. She was determined that Kelton wasn't going to spoil her lovely mood. She was happy and she was going to stay happy. No matter what he said.

When they got to her house, Kelton said grumpily, "I suppose you can open the door for yourself."

Laura wanted to laugh after the long lecture he'd given her about being a lady. She only said, "Thanks for the pizza and movie."

"You paid for the movie," he reminded her.

Laura did laugh a bit at that. She agreed, "Yes, I did. It was a wonderful movie too."

She ran lightly up the walk to her front porch. Kelton roared away before she was able to find the key and get in the front door. When she did get in, she was dismayed to find that there was still a light on in the kitchen. Had Gloria stayed up for her?

But it wasn't Gloria. It was her father. He was sitting at the kitchen table, leafing through a magazine. He looked up and said, "You're late."

Laura nodded and went to the refrigerator to pour herself a glass of milk. "We went to a party after the movie."

"I couldn't sleep." Her father yawned elaborately.

Laura knew that wasn't true. Her father could sleep anywhere, anytime. It was a family joke. But she said, "Too bad," as she waited for what was coming next.

"Understand you and your mother had a little row this afternoon."

"Yes, I was very rude to her. I'll apologize first thing tomorrow morning."

John Manning looked startled. He cleared his

throat and began again, "I want to talk to you about your relationship with your mother."

Laura's laughter rang out over the kitchen. She hugged her father and between laughs, explained, "I can't help it, Daddy. When you come at me with those canned speeches that I know you've been rehearsing all day. She did the same thing . . ." Laura collapsed against her arms and leaned her head on the kitchen table.

"Have you been drinking?" John Manning demanded suspiciously.

Laura wiped her eyes. "Is it so strange to hear me laugh? You're the second person who asked me that tonight. I don't drink. I don't intend to drink. Don't worry, Daddy."

Her father seemed perplexed but he plodded on. "I admit my message is canned, as you put it, but that doesn't make it less important. Gloria was very upset again tonight."

Laura put on a sober face and said, "I know and it *was* my fault. I'll apologize tomorrow. But I can't pretend. You don't want me to lie to her, do you?"

"I want your courtesy and cooperation. I want you to do the best you can to reconcile with your mother. I'd like you to make every effort . . ." John Manning looked miserable as he delivered his speech. Laura sipped a glass of milk quietly as she listened. It was difficult to preserve her happy mood, especially when he got to the part about how much he and Gloria appreciated her help. The way he talked, it was as if Gloria had been on a two-week vacation instead of a two-year desertion. Laura shook her head at her own anger and tried to remember how she felt when she was dancing with Don. It had been a good feeling.

After what seemed to be a long time, Laura said quietly, "All right, Dad. I'm going to try harder. I know you're right about Tommy. It isn't good for Tommy to be torn between Gloria and me. I will cooperate. Now, good-night." She kissed her father on the forehead and walked up the stairs to bed.

When she was ready to go to sleep, she closed her eyes and forced her mind to skip back over the evening, picking out the happy parts and dwelling on those. She thought about the warm feeling of friendship she'd felt when Marilyn called to her. She thought about her happiness at seeing Don. She thought, most of all, how it felt to be held in Don's arms again. Her last thought was, *He said he'd call tomorrow night.*

CHAPTER 11

Things went so smoothly the next two weekends that Gloria announced she would be moving home for good the next Friday. Laura smiled and said, "That's wonderful, Gloria. Maybe it will be all right if I go to Buffalo with Marilyn and Don? They're having the Northeastern States Final Marathon."

Gloria's face wavered between emotions and Laura was sure she was trying to decide whether or not to feel rejected. After a minute or two, she said, "I'm sure it will be nice, Laurie Baby."

"Gloria, it bothers me a lot when you call me Baby."

Her mother took a deep breath, pressed her lips together firmly into a small smile and said, "All right, Laura. I'll try to remember that."

Grateful that there hadn't been a scene, Laura smiled and softened the conversation by saying, "I know Tommy's thrilled to have you coming home sooner than we expected. He talked about it all week."

Gloria's face broke into a radiant smile. "We have so many plans for the summer. We're going sailing, swimming . . . how wonderful it is to feel well again."

Laura nodded politely. "Marilyn has invited me to share her room. She and Don will be competing against runners from four states. I'll be leaving right after school Friday and I won't be home till Sunday afternoon."

"Will you run?" Gloria asked.

Annoyed at her mother's ignorance, Laura spoke briefly. "No. This isn't an open marathon. Don and Marilyn have been partners in six races before this. The schools and Y's started the whole thing this year."

Gloria nodded. "I suppose it's because jogging is so popular."

"In a way," Laura agreed. She didn't bother to add that there was a difference between the sort of jogging overweight adults did on Sunday mornings and the long-distance marathon running that Don and Marilyn would do. Her mother wouldn't care anyway.

Gloria asked, "Do you want a new dress?"

"What for?"

"Won't there be a dance or a party? Wouldn't you like a new dress? We could shop together."

From the eagerness in Gloria's voice, Laura could tell she'd written a whole script about mother-daughter shopping. Laura shook her head and said, "If I want one, I'll buy it. I have plenty of money."

"Maybe I could help . . ." Gloria's voice trailed off and then she began again. "I suppose you've been choosing your own dresses for quite a while now."

Laura nodded her head, took an apple from the bowl of fruit on the kitchen table, and said, "Got to study."

"Want to come on a picnic with Tommy and me this afternoon?"

Laura shook her head. "Don and I are fixing up an old boat that belonged to his neighbor. If we can get it into shape, we'll take you and Tommy for a ride one of these days."

Laura left the room quickly, hoping that her quick refusal was covered with enough friendly banter to keep things working smoothly between Gloria and her. Even though she was trying very hard, she still found it difficult to be around Gloria for long without getting angry. Everytime she got angry she snapped at her mother, then Gloria reacted quickly with hurt feelings and tears.

Laura tried to stay away as much as possible on the weekends. Sometimes she felt like the White Rabbit running from one place to another, but it seemed the best way to handle things. It was fun being with Don again and that made it so much easier to avoid Gloria. Sometimes, when she had been talking with her mother for ten minutes or so, she felt as though she'd been walking on brittle ice. Things were smooth but they certainly weren't secure.

She was glad she was going to be gone the weekend that Gloria moved home permanently. It was easier not to watch Gloria bring her possessions in the door. Not that Gloria had that much. She didn't even have many clothes and several of the dresses she'd worn on weekend visits were ones Laura remembered from two and a half years ago.

Laura was thinking about her mother as she and Don and Marilyn drove toward Buffalo that Friday afternoon.

Marilyn said, "Hey, Laura, you're not listening. Are your thoughts worth a penny?"

"My mother moves in for good tonight," Laura answered.

Marilyn said, "That's a big adjustment. Scared?"

"Scared? Me scared? A little, I guess."

Don stretched his arms and shifted his weight slightly so that he could see out the window better. He waved his arm at the green fields on the right and said, "Your mother will be all right. Besides, it will be great to have the time free this summer. Nothing to be scared of."

Laura grinned. "Don, the only thing that would scare you would be a wild tiger on Main Street."

Marilyn shook her head. "No, that wouldn't scare him. He'd just walk up and say, 'How do you do, Mr. Tiger. Wouldn't you be more comfortable in your cage?' "

"And poor tiger, being totally bewildered by the sensible suggestion, would follow the Great Hunter Donald Douglas meekly down Main Street to his cage," Laura added mockingly.

Don looked from one girl to the other in bewilderment. He never teased and he didn't really seem to understand it when others teased him.

When they finally pulled into Buffalo, Don said, "Time to eat. Want to try this restaurant?"

"Let's look for a natural food restaurant," Laura said. "Not good for potential champions to eat junk food."

"You really prefer alfalfa sprouts to greasy hamburgers?" Marilyn teased her.

"I try to eat sensibly. It makes me feel good and my stomach is definitely better." She didn't add that having Don back in her life seemed to make it possible for her to drop the pills. She didn't like to think that she might be that dependent on anyone or anything for her happiness.

They found a natural food restaurant in the downtown section of Buffalo and ate a big dinner before checking into the hotel. It was difficult for Marilyn and Laura to go to sleep and they lay on their beds talking until almost midnight. Then Laura said, "We've got to stop talking. The race starts at nine-fifteen."

Marilyn said good-night and the room was silent for a while. Then Marilyn asked, "Laura, doesn't it make you . . . well, doesn't it make you kind of jealous to think that Don and I are running? You could have been in my place."

"Go to sleep," Laura answered. As she buried her head in the pillow, she thought about Marilyn's question. It was silly to worry about the past, wasn't it? At least that's what her mother and father were always saying, "Live one day at a time."

But the next morning, after she'd watched Don and Marilyn take off for the twenty-six-mile marathon, Laura felt at loose ends. There were a few other kids from high schools standing around with some officials and even some parents, but a marathon wasn't exactly the sort of thing you watched.

"Be fun to be a bird and follow along, wouldn't it?" one young man asked.

"Some of the others are taking a truck up to the halfway point," Laura offered.

He asked, "You going? By the way, my name's Alan Birkett."

"I'm Laura Manning. I'm going back to my room to read. I'll come back around noon."

The young man shook his head. "Too early. No one is going to finish in less than three and a half hours, you know."

"Probably not, but I'll be here when my friends come in. They're good."

"You have a special friend in the race?" Alan asked.

Laura nodded. He seemed like a nice fellow, but she didn't want to talk to him. Now that she was dating Don, she didn't want to do anything to jeopardize that relationship. Don had made it very clear that he couldn't tolerate any ups and downs or instability in their romance.

Since she needed Don's attention and support so desperately, Laura didn't want to take any chances. No sense encouraging Alan even though he was pleasant and attractive.

She spent the next three hours in her hotel lobby, leafing through old magazines, studying her chemistry, and finally reading a condensed version of a novel. At noon, she walked back to the high school track field that was the finish line of the race.

None of the runners were in sight, but a crowd was gathered. There were about one hundred people and Alan Birkett was one of them. He saw her and waved, but didn't try to join her. Laura edged up to a shady spot where she could see the finish line.

As she had hoped, Don was among the first three runners to finish the marathon. She ran up to him and said, "You've got a chance. Where's Marilyn?"

Don was still doing his slowing down exercises but he took time to say, "Don't know. Couldn't look backward." He was beginning to cool off some and began his stretching exercises. As he pulled on a sweatshirt, he added, "I think you're right. We've got a chance. She's pretty good."

The next two runners who came in were young women and Laura's heart sank as she saw that Marilyn wasn't one of them. It wasn't until she realized that neither of the young women was partner of the fellows who beat Don, that she cheered up. She said, "I think you've still got a chance."

"Maybe," he answered quietly. He was standing on the edge of the track, squinting into the sun. There were five or six figures clustered together and running toward them now. He said, "It's hard to tell. I think they're all fellows but one could be Marilyn. She's tall."

Laura jumped up and down and grabbed Don's arm. "There she is! There she is!"

Marilyn crossed the finish line and ran into the open arms of Don and Laura. The spectators realized that she was the first woman to join a partner. Within seconds, the officials made the announcement and Marilyn cut short her slowing down exercises to run to the judges' stand.

They handed Marilyn a large wooden plaque with a golden olive wreath attached to it. In the center of the wreath was a flaming torch of gold, and underneath were the words: FIRST SPECIAL RUNNING AWARD — NORTHEASTERN STATES.

Marilyn traced her finger along the olive wreath and said in a solemn voice, "This is the first thing I've ever won."

Laura reached out and touched the beautiful plaque. She said, "You're a champion."

Perhaps there was wistfulness in her voice because Marilyn burst into tears and threw her arms around Laura. She was crying and laughing at the same time, saying, "I'm sorry. I'm sorry." In the next breath, she laughed and said, "My mother will be so proud." Then she burst into tears again.

Don said, "You'd better get her to sit down in the shade, Laurie. I'll get the car. She's upset and exhausted."

Laura maneuvered Marilyn over to a bench in the shade and dipped a towel in cool water. As she was wiping off her friend's face, Alan Birkett, the young man she'd spoken to earlier, asked, "Is this your special friend?"

"One of them," Laura answered. "She's the new Northeastern Champion."

Marilyn burst into tears again and Laura started laughing at her.

Alan asked, "Does she do anything but run and sob?"

Marilyn and Laura both began laughing. Alan shook his head in mock amazement and then stuck out his hand. He said, "I'm Alan Birkett. Friend of your friend's. I've always wanted to meet a real champion. Beautiful too. You are very beautiful."

"How can you tell?" Marilyn asked innocently. She was wiping her face with the muddy towel again. Her hair, which had been braided tightly, was slicked back with sweat and her jogging suit which had been a glorious scarlet, was a dingy pink-grey because of the dust.

"I know beautiful when I see it. Would you have lunch with me?" Then, remembering his manners, he turned to Laura and included her in the invitation. "Both of you."

Laura was still laughing. She said, "I think Marilyn's not going to be in any shape for lunch. She needs a nap."

But Marilyn stood up decisively and said, "I'm fine. Alan, I'd love to have lunch with you. Pick me up in forty-five minutes?"

With that, Marilyn moved gracefully as a swan toward the Cadillac that Don was driving up the road. She turned and said, "We're at the Carlton." Then she smiled.

Laura was used to Marilyn's beauty, but even she was dazzled by that smile. She turned to look at Alan Birkett. What was it about the fellow that made Marilyn feel he deserved the full treatment? As far as Laura could see, he was just a tall, thin, ordinary guy.

But no matter what Laura thought, Marilyn was obviously taken with Alan. She didn't ask

Laura and Don to go along, so Laura pretended she'd rather be alone with Don.

When Don objected to the lunch date, saying she needed to rest, Marilyn said haughtily. "But some of the others are still running. I'm not tired. I'm a champion."

When Marilyn hadn't returned to the hotel by four, Don began to pace the floor. At four-thirty, he was pale and angry. At five, he wanted to call the police. Laura was worried, but Don was furious.

Marilyn walked into the hotel lobby at five-fifteen and Don jumped out of the lobby chair. He asked, "Where have you been?"

Marilyn smiled sweetly and said, "Alan took me to see the city. We went to a lovely place for lunch and then drove over to the river. I wish you'd been . . ." Marilyn stopped and asked Laura, "What's the matter with your friend?"

Laura answered, "He's been worried about you all afternoon. I think I should be jealous."

"Sweet," Marilyn said as she swept past them. "I'm going to pile all my hair on top of my head tonight. Maybe I'll braid it with some satin ribbons. It's wonderful to have such a tall escort."

"Are you going to the dinner with this Birkett?" Don demanded heavily.

"Yes, of course." Marilyn seemed amused that he'd asked.

"We don't know him," Don said. "All we know is that he tried to pick Laura up then you . . ."

"Don!" Laura interrupted.

"You don't know him but I do," Marilyn said with an amused expression. "He's a sophomore at Amherst and his brother ran in the marathon. He's going to be an ophthalmologist." She made a slight face at Don and said, "That should be stuffy enough to satisfy even you, Donald Douglas."

"It's not stuffy to worry about you," Don objected. "He's a complete stranger."

Laura poked Don in the ribs and said, "Lay off, Don. You're not her father."

Don looked slightly embarrassed as he said, "I'm sure he's fine, but we should double date."

Marilyn and Laura laughed loudly at the thought that it would have been any other way. When Marilyn saw that Don was getting red in the face, she said, "Don, I'm glad you're looking out for me. Don't be mad if we laugh at you a bit. Tell you what, just so you know I won't elope, you can drive tonight." Then she turned to Laura and winked. "I'd just as soon sit in the back seat."

Despite Don's fears, it was a wonderful evening and Laura was very glad that Marilyn had a date of her own. She'd often wondered if Don knew that Marilyn was interested in him. From his paternal reaction this afternoon, she understood that he thought of Marilyn as someone to be taken care of. Laura was glad Don didn't treat *her* like a child — at least most of the time he didn't.

They were dancing the last dance before Don mentioned the afternoon's incident. He began stiffly. "That Birkett seems all right. Think he'll call her again?"

"Yes, I think so. If not, it made this a very special evening."

"I guess you think I'm stuffy too."

Laura smiled and whispered in his ear, "Well, sometimes."

"I can't help being responsible. I've always been responsible. Someone has to be responsible."

Laura was taken aback. "Don, you sound really upset."

"I don't like being laughed at."

"Oh, Don, no one meant to hurt you," Laura said.

"I've never told you much about my childhood, Laurie. It was kind of awful. My mom and dad fought all the time and I . . . I was in the middle a lot. I tried to help my mother and then . . . it was as though I was always the adult in the family. There was a lot of violence. My mother was sort of simple, I guess, and my dad was just no good." There was bitterness in his voice as he said this. He added apologetically, "I know you think I don't have much of a sense of humor."

Laura was amazed that Don could sound so much like a hurt child. She understood now why he hadn't called her after the quarrel. She understood that Don was as scared and confused as she was. She said, "I understand the part about feeling like the adult in the family. I feel that way all the time. But the other part — the fights — must have been awful."

Don held her closer and said, "Awful. That's why I can't stand it when we fight. I try to remember that it isn't the same, but it's hard for me."

"My folks yelled at each other. There were a couple of embarrassing scenes, but that's all."

"You were lucky." Then Don laughed and said, "Not lucky. I guess no one is one hundred percent lucky, but there was a lot of stuff in my childhood I never talk about."

"You are a good person, Don. I'm sorry I laughed at you."

Don answered simply, "That's all right, Laurie. You're my girl. You can laugh at me if you want to."

CHAPTER 12

Don and Marilyn's picture was in the paper on Monday. The next Thursday, there was a long feature story about Marilyn Rogers, the beautiful and talented runner. Gloria showed Laura the clipping when she came home from school. "It could have been you," her mother said. "Oh, Laurie, I'm so sorry."

"If you could have seen the way Marilyn looked. She's so happy. Her mother is . . ." Suddenly Laura felt uncomfortable talking about mothers. She finished lamely, "Her mother is very, very happy for her."

Gloria said, "And you think Marilyn's mother is worth making happy, is that it?"

Laura put her cup of tea down firmly and went to her room. There was no sense in continuing a conversation with Gloria about mothers. She'd been home four days now, and each day she'd managed to find something to cry about. Laura's attempts to comfort her always ended with Laura feeling like a forty-year-old comforting an infant. Her mother was going to have to find some sort of balance without her support.

At dinner that night, Gloria brought the subject up again. She said, "Marilyn's picture looked so wonderful, but Laura is much prettier."

Laura smiled. "Really, Gloria, it's not necessary to tell me that I'm prettier than Marilyn. It wasn't a beauty contest."

Gloria's chin trembled and she had a quake in her voice. "I think you're much prettier than that gawky girl."

"Could we change the subject?"

Gloria rose from the table and threw her napkin on her plate, "I will not have you talk to me in this manner! You treat me as though I'm Tommy."

Laura looked at her coldly. She thought, that as a matter of fact, her mother was acting worse than Tommy.

When Gloria went to her room, John Manning gave Laura an exasperated look and followed his wife. Tommy immediately demanded dessert. Laura said, "You get no honey bars until you finish dinner."

Tommy grinned at Laura and said triumphantly, "Not honey bars tonight. Tonight we have Hostess Twinkies."

"Tommy," Laura groaned. "You know you're not allowed to eat that junk."

"Mama said I could."

"Don't you want to grow up to be strong and healthy?" Laura asked. When she saw the frightened and upset look on Tommy's face, she gave in. There was really no sense in putting poor Tommy in the middle of things. She said, "Don't take advantage of Gloria too often. It will rot your teeth."

As Laura was giving Tommy his Twinkies, John Manning came back to the table long enough to ask, "Will you do the dishes? Your mother is going to lie down a few minutes before she goes to the A.A. meeting."

Laura asked, "Are you going out? I was meeting Don at the library."

"Sorry," her father said swiftly. Laura could tell by the way he was talking to her that he held her responsible for the upset at dinner. "I have a client and your mother has to go to a meeting every night for a while. Maybe Don could come over here."

Tears rushed to Laura's eyes. Having Gloria home hadn't really changed things so much after all. She still had to keep things together around the house and be responsible for Tommy.

Don seemed happy enough to spend the evening at the Manning household. He helped with the dishes and then ate some of the honey bars Tommy had turned down. He told the boy, "You're crazy. These are a whole lot better. Got nuts, raisins, and honey."

"Really?" Tommy asked. He looked at the honey bars and then back to the two packages of Twinkies. It was clear that he was torn between loyalties. He settled it by saying, "I'll have both."

Don laughed, but Laura didn't. After Tommy was put to bed, she said to Don, "I'm really worried about him. He seems so confused about what to do. The dessert tonight was just one example."

"Give him time, Laurie." Don leaned back

against the arm of the chair and flipped through his physics book. "Will you quiz me?"

Laura looked down at Don's bright red hair and smiled. She said, "You look like a little kid yourself, sitting on the floor with a glass of milk and cookies. Sure you're old enough for physics?"

It was almost the exact question that Gloria asked them when she came in from the A.A. meeting. She stood in the doorway and asked, "Sure you're old enough to read? You look so young down there on the floor."

Laura felt the old resentment stir in her. Funny how Gloria could make her so angry so quickly. She supposed her father was right. She probably was touchy.

Don stood up and asked, "How was the meeting, Mrs. Manning?"

Gloria came in and sat down in a chair. "Could you call me Gloria?" she asked Don. "Laura's called me that ever since she could talk."

Gloria reached over and tousled Laura's hair as she smiled down at her daughter. "For a minute, I thought you were a toddler again. You looked so sweet."

Laura stood up. She asked, "Would you like some tea?"

Gloria's face took on that hurt, childish look again, and she shook her head. "I'll go to bed."

Don said, "Don't leave, Gloria. Tell us about the meeting. Was it a good one?"

Gloria looked at Don gratefully and sat back in her chair. "We're not supposed to talk about anyone who was there or what anyone said, but, yes, it was a good meeting. Very good. I don't know what I'd do without them."

"Is it difficult to switch groups?" Don asked. "The Pittsfield meetings must be different from the ones at Serenity Farm."

Gloria answered, "Different in some ways, but A.A. is the same all over the world. We've got a million alcoholics who learned to stay sober through A.A. now. There are groups in Mexico and Europe and just all over . . . even Africa."

Laura brought in three teas. She sat quietly and listened as Gloria told Don all about the A.A. program. As Gloria talked, Laura grew more and more jealous. Don treated Gloria with the same gentle attention that her father did.

What was it about Gloria that made them think she had to be treated like a China doll? She was tough enough, as far as Laura could see. In four days, she'd managed to destroy two years of discipline for Tommy and cause a real breach between Laura and her father. Laura watched her mother shimmer and sparkle under Don's attention. No — Gloria was no fragile flower. Gloria was smarter than most of the men in the world. Gloria was . . . well . . . Gloria was her mother, so she wouldn't even think about what Gloria was.

Suddenly, Laura felt very, very old and very, very tired. She was sick of watching Gloria ruin everything. First her dad, then Tommy, and now Don. She stood up and said, "I'm tired. I'm going to bed."

Don and Gloria looked surprised but they kept right on talking as she walked up the stairs to her bedroom. They were still talking when her father came in at eleven. The last thing she heard was her mother saying to her father as they walked up the stairs, "I don't know why you think he's stuffy. He's a wonderful boy."

CHAPTER 13

Dinner went smoothly the next night and Gloria seemed very cheerful. It was a relief to everyone, but Laura couldn't get over the feeling that living with Gloria was a bit like living with a spontaneous combustion machine. She seemed to erupt into confusion, tears, or anger at least once a day.

That night, Gloria announced, "I'm not going to a meeting tonight. I went at noon so we could all be together."

"I wish I'd known," Laura grumbled. "Don and I might have gone to the movies."

"It will do us good to be together as a family," John Manning said quickly. "We'll pop some corn and watch television."

"I have to study," Laura said.

When her mother's face took on that hurt, childish expression, Laura's father spoke, "No, Laura. No books tonight. We'll spend the evening as a family. It will be a first."

Laura wanted to remind him that before Gloria arrived, she'd been the one to insist on family evenings. In truth, her dad would rather show real estate than sit home and watch television. But it would do no good to remind her father of the past. He was clearly blinded by the novelty of having Gloria home.

Gloria seemed as delighted by the fantasy family life as her husband was. After dinner, she changed into a new hostess robe and settled down on the sofa next to her husband. When Tommy snuggled in between them, Laura felt like an outsider.

She sat in the wing chair in front of the television set and pretended to be interested in the movie. Every few minutes she would get up and get a drink or make some tea. Finally her father said, "Laura, sit down and watch this. It's good."

Laura felt like a ten-year-old who had been reprimanded. It was humiliating to be put in this position just because her mother returned. After all, before Gloria came back, it was she — Laura — who had made all the decisions around the house. Her father made her sick with all this new-found family-man image of his.

Gloria ate popcorn and laughed delightedly at the screen. During the commercials, she turned to Laura and tried to force conversation. Laura answered in monosyllables, but Gloria and her father seemed determined not to notice. Tommy was obviously having the time of his life.

At nine, Laura said, "Bedtime, Tommy."

He turned to Gloria and asked, "Can't I stay up?"

"Your bedtime is nine," Laura reminded him.

"I don't want to."

"Go to bed," Laura snapped.

When Tommy turned from his mother to his father for help, there were tears in his eyes. Gloria, who was obviously torn between trying to cooperate with Laura's rules and wanting to please Tommy, gave her daughter an appealing look.

Laura was furious. Her mother had agreed not to go against the house rules. Laura shook her head to the unspoken request and reminded all three of them, "Tommy's bedtime is nine. If he stays up later, he's tired and cranky all day Saturday."

Gloria spoke up, "It's a special occasion."

Laura ignored Gloria and said to Tommy, "Go to bed."

The child got up obediently and kissed his mother and father good-night. He hugged his mother an extra-long time. "Laura's right. I *am* cranky if I stay up too late." He did not kiss Laura good-night as he left the room.

Laura leaned back in the chair. At least Tommy had had the good sense to follow house rules. Her two years training had some fruit after all. As for his not kissing her, it was clear that he was torn between his childish desire to please his mother and his adult knowledge of what was best. He had made the best compromise he could.

Gloria apparently didn't think so. "Laura, you are driving Tommy away from you by your rigid attitudes."

Laura turned to her mother in amazement. The anger and resentment she'd tried to hold back all week flowed out. "*I'm* driving him away? I'm not the one who switches rules every minute. I'm not the one who gives in to his whims. Grow up,

Gloria. You're the one who's trying to destroy two years of discipline and reasonable upbringing. You're trying to buy Tommy's love."

Gloria burst into tears and cried, "Every move I make in this house, you're standing there criticizing me! You tell me how to cook! You tell me how to clean! How to raise my own child! I'm sick of it and I'm going . . . I can't stand it. I can't stand it!" She ran from the house, sobbing as though her heart would break.

Laura leaned back and yawned. Her mother's scenes were getting too tiresome. She was sick of the whole thing and maybe it would be better if her mother did leave. Two women in the house were too many.

This time, John Manning didn't follow his wife. Instead, he yelled at Laura, "Get that smirk off your face!"

Laura's head snapped back as though she'd been slapped. She felt betrayed by her father's unreasonable anger. How could he forget all she had done for him? How could he ignore the two years of love and attention she'd given him and Tommy? What right had her father to speak to her like that?

Somehow, having her father turn on her, was more than Laura could bear. The same words ran through her head, over and over. *After all I've done* . . . and . . . *he doesn't love me at all*.

Through her tears, she sobbed, "You don't care anything at all about me. Do you?"

He was still yelling as he answered, "I've told you over and over that you're to treat Gloria gently. You take every opportunity to make trouble. Can't you see that she's on the verge of drinking again? You have to be careful."

"I ran this household for two years and no one worried about me. No one hovered over me every minute, asking how I felt, asking if I was tired. She's not as fragile as you think and she's ruining everything." Laura squeezed the tears back. She was determined not to cry anymore.

"You didn't run this household, I did! And I'm still in charge here. Now get this through your head. I'm the parent and you're the child. What I say goes and I say you treat Gloria gently — very gently."

"And what about Tommy?" Laura asked. "Are you saying Tommy can do as he pleases now? Do you realize how hard I've worked to give him a sense of security? Do you realize how confused he was when she left? Doesn't anything count for you?"

"I'm not talking about the past," her father roared. "I'm talking about the future. You're never to talk to your mother that way again. We've got to be careful . . . very careful."

Laura felt a mixture of feelings — all bad. She felt angry at her father and angry at Gloria, and angry at herself for getting involved in this situation again. She mostly felt hurt and rejected, though. It took everything she had to make an exit from that room without breaking into hysterics the way Gloria had.

As she climbed the stairs, she bit her lips to keep from crying out at the pain she felt. She didn't know when she had last felt this confused and frightened. Yes, she did know. Suddenly, she remembered the night Gloria had left home. As clearly as anything, she could see her mother standing at the bottom of the stairs, weaving from side to side, her words a jumble of confused anger and self-pity. Laura had stood at the top of the stairs and held Tommy close as her father chased his wife out into the street, begging her to return.

Laura understood that her father was terrified that they would replay that scene. She understood his terror but she couldn't forgive him for turning on her. She would never forgive him for the cruel and heartless way he had treated her tonight.

Laura passed Tommy's door and he called out to her. She stopped and went in. He asked in a small, frightened voice, "Is she all right?"

Laura nodded and smoothed the hair off Tommy's forehead. Even her little brother was more concerned about Gloria than her. The world felt like a cruel and heartless place as she went into her own room and closed the door.

Laura lay on the bed, looking at the ceiling and thinking about her situation. She thought about it until two in the morning but she could come up with nothing new. As she went over Gloria's childish behavior and — most of all — her father's betrayal, she felt only bitterness.

At two-thirty, Laura got up and packed her suitcase. She chose a selection of her most adult clothes. If she wanted the situation changed, there seemed to be no other way to change it. Either she or her mother was going to have to go, and clearly her father and Tommy would prefer that Gloria stay. That was all right. She had almost three hundred dollars, which she'd saved over the last two years from the erratic allowance her father gave her. It was enough to get to New York City and rent a room at the Y while she looked for a job.

Comforted by the thought that she could always run away, Laura dozed off. In the morning, she would go to the bank and she would have her money ready. With her bag packed and her money in her pocket, Laura would be able to leave the house whenever things got any tougher. She fell asleep with a smile on her face as she thought of her freedom of choice. Somehow, it restored her sense of dignity to have a plan.

Laura didn't wake until nine-thirty the next morning. She rubbed her eyes and checked her alarm. Someone had pushed the plunger in. Annoyed that Gloria or her father had seen fit to break her date with Don, she dressed quickly and went into the kitchen.

Gloria looked up from her newspaper and asked cheerfully, "Have a good sleep?"

How her mother could have those hysterical fits one minute and be so cheerful the next, Laura didn't understand. She didn't say anything about it though. Instead, she turned to Tommy and said, "Sugar Smacks? Where did you get them?"

"Mama bought them for me," Tommy said defensively. Then he added, "But I'll eat oatmeal too."

Gloria broke in. "We were out of oatmeal so I found these on the shelf."

"If you found them on the shelf, you put them there," Laura said coldly, as she pulled the dead leaves off her geraniums. Since Gloria's arrival, her flowers were dying, one by one. "Junk foods weren't permitted until you came home."

"I see a night's sleep hasn't cured your grumps," Gloria said. "It has mine. I'm sorry I'm so moody. They tell me it's a normal part of recovery. I'll get more emotional balance soon. And it won't be long before I'll be able to go to one or two meetings a week instead of going every night."

"Good." Laura poured herself a mixture of yeast, dry milk, yogurt, and orange juice.

"Ugh!" Gloria said. "How do you stand that stuff?"

Laura put the glass down on the table top and said slowly and carefully, "Some people put real poison in their bodies. I try to drink what's good for me."

Gloria dropped the coffee cup she was rinsing, and as it crashed, she picked up a plate and threw it across the room. She was screaming as she threw the second plate. "You're driving me out! You're trying to make me drink! I can't stand it any longer!"

Gloria rushed to the kitchen door and Laura stood up at the same time. She said, "No you don't. This time you clean up your own mess. I'm sick of cleaning up after you. Pick it up yourself."

Gloria stopped and stared at Laura. She asked, "You really hate me, don't you?"

"Help Tommy," Laura said coldly.

Gloria turned and saw that Tommy was trying to pick up the pieces of cups and plates that lay strewn across the floor. Gloria ran to her son and hugged him, smoothing down his hair, rocking him back and forth. "Tommy, Tommy, Mommy's sorry she lost her temper. Mommy's sorry."

Laura felt nothing but disgust at the sight of the two of them, holding on to each other and picking up pieces of broken pottery. She watched for a moment and then decided to put her plan in action. Nothing was going to get better around here. It was only getting worse.

Quickly and quietly, she went upstairs, got her suitcase, and walked out the front door. Gloria and Tommy were still in the kitchen and they didn't even hear her leave. That was all right. *They won't miss me*, she thought.

She carried the suitcase to the small grocery store two blocks away, where she went inside and asked, "Mrs. Jennings, do you mind if I leave this suitcase here? I have to go downtown and then my friend will pick me up. I won't be an hour."

Mrs. Jennings, busy with her crossword puzzles as always, nodded and asked perfunctorily, "Going on a trip?"

"Just overnight to a cousin's in Chatham, but my dad isn't home. I think my friend will pick me up in her car."

The store proprietor seemed satisfied with the explanation, even though the suitcase was too large for an overnight trip. Laura had counted on this woman to be too engrossed in her hobby to be curious, and she had been right. *If only Mr. Brewster at the bus station did crosswords*, Laura thought. But Mr. Brewster's hobby was gossiping. She had to find some other way to get out of town besides taking the bus.

Laura stood in line at the bank behind a teller

she didn't know, so she wouldn't have to tell any more lies. She left ten dollars in her account so there would be no reason for anyone to question her.

By eleven-thirty, she'd taken her money out of the bank and called Kelton. She picked up her suitcase and was waiting for him at the corner at two-thirty. When he pulled up in his father's brand-new car, Laura said, "I appreciate this, Kelton. I really do."

Kelton looked at the suitcase and smiled. "I thought you said you were going for the weekend."

"I am, but my cousin's house in Albany is full of children. They're kind of poor so I'm bringing some of Tommy's hand-me-downs."

Kelton said nothing more except, "It was a surprise to hear from you. You and Don have another fight?"

"Sort of," Laura said. She didn't want to have to invent any big lies. If this disappearance of hers was going to work, she didn't want to say more than she had to.

She figured her folks would call Don and Marilyn first thing. It would probably be days before they found out Kelton drove her to Albany. By that time, she would be lost in New York City. No one would ever find her there. She would be on her own.

CHAPTER 14

Kelton seemed to be delighted to drive her to Albany. He talked a mile a minute about himself, his plans, and successes, and his grades. About twenty miles outside Pittsfield, he asked, "How about stopping for a drink before we get to town?"

Laura agreed. If she was going to cover her tracks carefully, she would have to spend the afternoon with Kelton. After all, when she'd called him, she'd invited him to dinner. It was the only way she could think to get out of town. If she'd taken a bus from Pittsfield, Mr. Brewster, the ticket master, would have been on the phone to her folks within five minutes.

Kelton swung into a roadside diner and they got out. He said, "It's hot. I could go for a beer."

The diner was really more of a bar than a restaurant. It had a counter at one end, but Kelton led the way to the side room that was darkly lit and had soft leather seats in the booths. Laura sat down and Kelton sat beside her. She wanted to ask him to sit on the other side but didn't know how to. When the waitress came, Kelton ordered a beer and Laura ordered some orange juice.

As the waitress left, Kelton asked, "Want some Vodka in that juice? This is New York State. You could pass for eighteen."

Laura shook her head. "I don't drink."

Kelton laughed loudly at that. He seemed to find it very funny.

Laura, who had been so concerned about her problems, hadn't really let Kelton bother her before. Now she asked, "What's so funny?"

Kelton gulped the beer and motioned to the waitress for another one. "You must admit it's a bit unusual, considering your background."

Laura decided to play it straight. She said, "It's the most sensible thing to do. Children of alcoholics are high-risk candidates for the same disease."

"What disease?"

"Alcoholism."

Kelton smiled in that superior way of his. "Oh, yes, the mysterious disease of alcoholism. Laura, you don't really buy that garbage, do you?"

Laura shifted uncomfortably in her seat. In truth, she did have a hard time accepting that alcoholism was a disease instead of lack of will power. She'd taken Kelton's point of view more than once when she argued with Don. Finally, Don had said, "If the statements of the American Medical Association aren't enough for you, then have it your own way."

That was one of the times when Laura had felt that Don was deliberately taking her mother's side. Now she was running away from home, sitting in a dark bar with a young man she didn't like, and defending her mother. "There's no other explanation for the way some people continue to drink long after they find out it's bad for them."

Kelton smiled again and shifted so that his leg rubbed against hers. He dropped an arm around her shoulder and hugged her lightly as he said in a low voice, "Come on, Laura. People drink to have a good time. Don't you think a beautiful woman like your mother was having the time of her life in that big city?"

Laura moved away from Kelton and laughed self-consciously. "Let's just change the subject, Kelton."

Kelton squeezed over closer. He said, "Laura, let's talk about you and me." He leaned his head up next to hers and whispered, "Call those cousins and say you'll be late. Spend the night with me, Laura."

Laura froze when she heard his suggestion. *What possible right?* Then she understood. She said in a sharp voice, "Like mother, like daughter. Is that what you're thinking, Kelton? Well, you don't know a thing about my mother and you know less about me. Now let's get out of here before I get mad."

Kelton put his arm around her tighter and said, "You're not in any position to get mad, Laura. You need to be nice to me. You need me."

Laura poked him in the ribs with her elbow. "Kelton, this is ridiculous. Let me out of this stupid corner." She tried to laugh, to smooth the whole thing over.

Kelton shook his head and squeezed her arm.

He spoke in a voice that was a cross between a whisper and a hiss, "You're a pretty girl, Laura. But you're not too bright. You think I don't know you're running away? You think I don't know why you're carrying that big suitcase?"

"I told you it was clothes for my cousin. Now let's go. This dark place is turning you into a vampire or something else weird enough for the late-late movie."

Laura, who was pinned against the wall, tried to get up. Kelton pulled her down beside him and said, "You want to be nice to me, Laura. I might blow your whole plan."

Cold fury in her voice, Laura said, "Kelton, let go of me. If you don't let me out of this ridiculous corner right now, I'm going to call for help."

Kelton must have understood she was serious. He pulled away from her, slid out of the booth, and stood up. His eyes were embarrassed and angry as he said, "You think I'm a fool? You think I don't know why you asked me to drive you instead of Don? You think I don't know you were using me, Laura? You're a lot like your mother, Laura. You look like her and you're going to end up like her. Using men isn't very nice."

"You don't know a thing about my mother," Laura said coldly. She reached for the bill, laid five dollars on the table, and walked to the door. When they got to the car, she said, "Give me my suitcase. I'll get to my cousin's some other way."

Kelton opened the trunk, dumped her suitcase on the ground, jumped in his car, and roared away.

Laura looked at the retreating car, wondering how she would get to Albany from here. She shivered in the early evening air, picked up her suitcase, and walked back inside the diner. There was nothing else around so she had no other choice.

She carried the heavy bag inside the door and asked the waitress, "Is there a bus to Albany from here?"

The waitress shook her head. "No bus."

"How about a taxi?"

"Cost you about forty dollars," the waitress volunteered. "Maybe if you hang around, you can hitch a ride with Jake Shepard. He usually stops here for dinner. Nice guy. You'd be safe."

Laura nodded wearily and sat down at the counter of the diner. She said, "I'd like some scrambled eggs and a glass of milk, please." It was the first food she'd eaten today and her stomach was beginning to complain.

Four hours later, the waitress said to her, "I guess Jake's not coming. Sorry, kid, I'd drive you to Albany myself, but my kids are waiting."

Laura looked again at the clock on the diner wall. It was almost nine o'clock. She said, "I guess I'd better call that cab or I'll never get there."

"Too bad you're not going to Pittsfield," the waitress said. "I could give you a ride there."

Laura thought about going back to Pittsfield with this woman and then taking the bus from there to Albany or New York, but there might not be any more busses leaving tonight. Somehow, she had the feeling that if she turned around, she'd never get away. She said, "I'll call the cab."

"Good girl. We close at ten so tell him to hurry."

The taxi arrived at five minutes of ten and Laura was in Albany by ten-forty. The ride only cost twenty-eight dollars and she was sorry she'd waited so long to call. Even so, she'd only been on the road a half a day and her three hundred dollars was closer to two hundred and fifty. The gas and drinks she'd bought Kelton put the first bite in it and now the taxi ride. *Two hundred and fifty dollars won't last long in New York City,* Laura worried.

She tried to clear her doubts from her tired and depressed mind as she asked the ticket seller, "What time is the next bus to New York?"

"Just missed it," the ticket seller said.

Laura's heart sank. She looked around the bus station at the empty seats, the littered floors, and the three lone travelers waiting. She asked, "How about Boston?"

"Make up your mind," the ticket seller said. His eyes narrowed suspiciously and he asked, "Where do you want to go?"

Color flooded Laura's face as she stumbled over her words. "New York. I'm going to New York. I just wondered if I could get there by way of Boston." If there was anything she didn't need, it was to have the ticket seller call the police and ask if they were looking for a teenage run-away.

He shook his head curtly and answered, "No bus to no place. First thing out is five in the morning."

She opened her purse and said, "One-way ticket to New York City, please."

"Can't get out until tomorrow morning."

Laura set her lips firmly and said, "I'll wait."

The ticket seller's eyes followed her as she walked away from the window and over to the small refreshment stand. Laura told herself to relax and not be nervous, that it was natural that he would look at her. She was sure that she looked old enough to be traveling. After all, sixteen and eighteen weren't that far apart, and she was wearing her golden blonde hair pulled up in a knot.

She ordered a cup of coffee and a doughnut at the refreshment stand, then ploughed through the rack of paperbacks. Even though she wanted to watch her money, she knew she would have to have something to read. It was a long time from midnight till five in the morning. She bought a current bestseller that looked fat enough to keep her occupied.

As she handed the snack bar attendant money for the coffee and book, he said, "Wouldn't think a pretty girl like you would be interested in reading."

Laura didn't bother to answer him. She was beginning to understand that being on your own in a big city at night was touchy, if not dangerous. She certainly didn't want to do anything to encourage this man.

Apparently sitting alone in a bus station at night was all the encouragement anyone needed. Between midnight and two, Laura was accosted by the ticket seller, the snack bar attendant, one sailor on leave, and two drunks. After she threatened the second drunk with calling the police, she was close to tears. When he laughed and sat down next to her, saying, "No girl like you wants the police, honey," Laura walked to the phone booth and put a dime in.

She intended to call information or a fake number but instead, she found herself fishing in her wallet for Jerri Hill's number.

"Hello?" The voice at the other end was sleepy.

"Hi, Jerri, this is Laura Manning. I don't know if you remember me."

"Laura! Of course I remember you. How are you?" Jerri's voice was warm and friendly.

Tears began streaming down Laura's face. She said, "Not too good, I guess. I had a fight with my father."

"Are you home?" Jerri's voice cut across the wire quickly.

Laura laughed self-conciously. "No. I'm in Albany. At the bus station. It's silly, I suppose, but you told me I could call you anytime."

"You're in the bus station alone?" Jerri's voice was incredulous.

"Yes."

"Laura, I'll be there in fifteen minutes. I'm close."

"You don't have to do that."

"Wait for me," Jerri said and hung up.

Laura stared at the dead phone and wondered why she'd called Jerri. Now she would have to listen to lectures about why she should go home. Feeling worse than ever, Laura considered leaving before Jerri got there. But that would be crazy. Where would she go at three in the morning?

The drunk she'd been avoiding wandered away, so Laura went back to her suitcase and sat down on the bench in a daze. She was so numb and tired that she wasn't really in any condition to make any more decisions. *I'll just talk to Jerri a while and get on the bus. There's no need to panic.*

But Laura's heart was beating fast and her pulse was racing when Jerri got there. The first thing she said was, "I'm not going home."

Jerri grinned at her and stuck her hands in the windbreaker she'd thrown over her flannel shirt. She said, "I know the feeling. Remember, I left home at thirteen. By my standards, you should have flown the coop a long time ago."

Relief flooded Laura's face as she said, "I'm glad you approve. It was just awful. Ever since Gloria got there, we've been in a mess."

"Been a rough two weeks, huh, kid?" Jerri asked softly.

Laura was stunned. She smiled shyly and said, "Two weeks? It feels more like two years. I guess you think I should give it a longer try? That's what Don always tells me."

"Don?"

"He's my boyfriend. He takes Gloria's side all the time too. They're all against me. I feel, I feel . . ." Tears rolled down Laura's face in washes of grief.

Jerri reached in her pocket and said, "I left in a hurry but I remembered Kleenex. Blow."

It was kind of nice crying as Jerri watched. She didn't seem to be in a hurry to stop Laura's tears and she didn't seem too upset. A couple of times, she made encouraging sounds and when Laura seemed to be finished, she said, "I guess you have a hard time doing that."

"What?"

"Crying. You don't strike me as the sort who can cry easily. More the grin-and-bear-it type, I'd guess."

Laura sniffled. "I'm usually much more grown-up, but lately I've been very emotional. I yelled at my mom and then at my dad. I guess I'm just feeling sorry for myself." Laura sobbed loudly and picked up some fresh Kleenex from the pile Jerri had put in her lap.

"If you don't, who will? I feel sorry for you too, Laura."

"You do?"

"Does that surprise you?" Jerri laughed. "Don't forget I'm the child of an alcoholic. It's not easy for you or Gloria. I also envy you because you seem to know a lot of things intuitively that it took me years to learn. You're a special person."

"Special. That's what the Judge told me. Marilyn too."

Jerri nodded warmly. "Lots of people admire you. Love you too."

Laura turned this over in her mind. "Love me?" She ran through her list of relatives and friends. Clearly her mom and dad were too involved with each other to really love her. Don — well maybe what Don felt for her could develop into love. Aloud, she said, "Tommy loves me."

"Another boyfriend?"

"My little brother." At the thought of Tommy, Laura crumpled into another round of sobbing.

Jerri waited while Laura cried. Sometimes she handed Laura more Kleenex. After a long time, Laura said, "I've got to go back home. Who will look after Tommy?"

Jerri nodded. "You know what's best, Laura. I think in time you may find that Gloria and your father also love and need — " When Laura shook her head vehemently, Jerri broke off. She asked, "Do you need return fare?"

Laura laughed loudly at that, rubbing her swollen and red eyes with the back of her hand. She said, "When Gloria was away — all the time she was away — Tommy insisted she'd come back her 'return fare.' I wonder if he's waiting the same someday. He kept saying she just needed to get way for me right now?"

Jerri pointed to the clock on the wall. "You've only got an hour and a half before you're on your way home. You can ask him then. Now, how about if I spring for breakfast. I know an all-night restaurant that we can go to."

Laura stood up. "I'd love that, but I'm buying. I have plenty of money."

"Then you can plan to come back and see me often. It's only an hour and a half on the bus, you know."

"Sure." She laughed again. "I've been on the road since ten-thirty this morning and I'm only one hour and a half away from Pittsfield. Not much progress."

"Maybe more than you know," Jerri said softly. "Maybe a lot more than you know."

CHAPTER 15

Laura slept on the short bus trip to Pittsfield but it didn't help much. She entered the front door of her home, feeling exhausted, embarrassed, and defiant all at the same time. Opening the door quietly, she slipped into the living room and turned to go up the stairs.

It was only six-forty and there was always the possibility that she could get to her room without being noticed. It could be that her folks wouldn't know she was gone. It could be that they would think she'd spent the night with Marilyn or been out late with Don. It was with that faint hope that she'd rented a locker at the Pittsfield bus station and stored her suitcase.

But Laura wasn't up two steps before she heard her mother screaming at her father, "And I've told you over and over, I don't know where she is!"

Laura turned around and went toward the kitchen but she stopped in the doorway, where she could see her parents. Her father's back was turned. He was standing over Gloria, who was slumped over a cup of coffee with her arms crossed in front of her and her head hung low. Though Gloria raised her head slightly to talk with her husband, she didn't see Laura. She said, "We have to call the police, John."

John Manning lifted his arm as though he was going to strike his wife. His voice was tight and horrible as he said, "We will *not* call the police, Gloria. Laura is sensible. If she's gone out for the night — for whatever reason — she'll come home. She's not a child."

"You think I'm the child," Gloria said. Her words were muffled in her arms as she lay her head down on the table.

"I think if anything happens to Laura, I will never, never forgive you," John Manning said.

Laura's heart beat so quickly she thought it would break. *He does care about me*, she thought. Suddenly, the exhaustion and the long heartbreaking trip seemed worth it. She didn't even mind coming home in defeat. It was all worth it to know her father did love her after all.

Gloria stood up, picked up her purse, and said, "Nor shall I ever forgive myself." She pulled on her sweater and walked to the kitchen door.

"Where do you think you're going?" John Manning asked.

"Out for a while," Gloria answered. She turned and opened the door.

Her husband called after her, "If you think I'm going to beg you to stay this time, you're wrong."

From outside, Laura heard her mother say, "*You're* wrong, John. I don't want you to beg me to stay. I'm not even leaving because you're obviously looking for someone to take all the blame.

I'm leaving because I'm sick of being treated like a child."

"You are a child," John Manning answered. He was shouting as he called, "That girl of mine had more sense when she was ten than you do now."

Faintly, Laura heard her mother retort, "She's my daughter too."

Laura climbed the stairs to her bedroom. She would have liked to run and comfort her father but she told herself she was too tired. There would be time enough for comforting him later. Right now, she needed rest. It felt good to be home and know that her father and Tommy loved her. She lay down top of her bed and within seconds she was sound asleep.

It was a good sleep but a short one. At eight-thirty, Tommy woke her. He was shouting, "Mama, Daddy, Laura's back! Laura's back!"

He jumped onto the bed and grabbed her face between his hands. One knee poked her in the ribs and the other pinned down her arm. Laura groaned. "Tommy, get off me."

John Manning appeared in the doorway. He asked, "When did you get in?"

Laura sat up in bed and yawned and stretched. She said, "Late, I was out late. We went to the movies in Albany and then we had a flat tire."

John Manning shook his head. "Won't work, Laura. Don was the one who was most frantic. He was here until three."

"Where's Mama?" Tommy demanded. "I want to tell her Laura's home." He stopped in the doorway long enough to tell Laura, "She cried a lot when she found out you were gone. She loves you."

"Your mother's gone shopping," John Manning said.

"Shopping?" Tommy's face showed bewilderment. "When will she be home?"

"I'm not sure," his father answered. There was a tired, older look about his face. He smiled at his son and said, "Nothing to worry about, son. She'll be back soon. Meanwhile, we have a baseball game."

Tommy's face closed over. He said, "She promised to go too."

Laura was afraid that Tommy was going to cry. She jumped out of bed and hugged him closely. "Don't worry, Tommy. Gloria had to go out. You go to the baseball game with Daddy. She'll probably be home before you are."

But Tommy was crying and continued demanding, "Where's Mama? I want Mama to come home too."

"Stop crying," John Manning said in a loud voice.

At the sound of his father's order, Tommy began wailing at the top of his lungs. John Manning looked helplessly at Laura and then back to Tommy. He threatened, "If you don't stop crying right now, you'll have to go to your room."

Laura stepped between her father and Tommy as she said smoothly, "He's tired. You know he gets like this when he stays up too late. Why don't you go play golf and Tommy and I will bake cookies."

Her father looked at her gratefully and kissed her on the forehead. "Thanks, Laura, I'll be home in time for supper."

After her father was gone, Laura knelt down and spoke softly to Tommy. "Tommy, Tommy, listen to me. You're all right. I'm home and you're all right. Now, how about baking some cookies together? Wouldn't that be fun?"

Tommy nodded his head and said in a small voice, "I was afraid. Afraid you'd gone away, Laura."

Impulsively, Laura hugged her small brother to her. "It's all right, Tommy. I'm not leaving. We're going into the kitchen now and we'll make chocolate chips if you want."

"I'd rather have honey bars," Tommy said.

Laura laughed delightedly and hugged him closer. "That's my boy. It's going to be just like old times."

CHAPTER 16

Don was there before they put the cookies in the oven. He listened quietly as Laura explained that she'd been to Albany to talk with Jerri. She didn't tell him she'd been running away, nor did she tell him about Kelton. Somehow, that concerned look on Don's face made her feel too ashamed. The more she thought of Saturday night's escapade, the more childish she felt.

He drank his coffee quietly and listened to her story. Then he said, "I'm glad you're home, Laurie. I know you've been having a rough time and I was afraid you'd done something foolish."

"Foolish?" Laura laughed and asked, "What did you think I'd done?"

He answered, "I don't know. Ran off with a sailor, maybe."

Laura blushed as she remembered that dreadful bus terminal and the men who had approached her. One had been a sailor on leave. To her, Don's joke was no joke.

He continued, "You might think I'm stodgy but you'd be surprised how imaginative I really am. I can run regular horror movies in my mind when my girl disappears."

Laura knew he wasn't kidding in spite of the jesting tone. *He really cares about me,* Laura thought. It was a warm and wonderful feeling. In a way, she was glad she'd run away because she'd discovered the depth of feeling that Tommy, her father, and Don had for her.

Gloria called on the telephone just then and when Laura answered the phone, her mother said, "You're home. Thank God."

"I'm home." Her good mood seemed to shatter into a thousand pieces. Soon her mother would return and the battle would begin again.

Gloria must have sensed that Laura wasn't exactly overjoyed to hear from her. She asked, "May I speak to John?"

"Golfing," Laura answered shortly.

"Golfing!" Her mother screamed the word in Laura's ear. Then she asked in a more controlled voice, "Are you sure?"

"I'm sure," Laura answered coldly. She added, "I have to take my cookies out of the oven."

The phone clicked in her ear. Laura turned back to Don and asked, "Did you get any work done on the boat?"

"Laura, I was up till three-thirty worrying about you."

She pulled the cookies from the oven. "I'm home now and here's your reward for worrying."

Don took a cookie and poured himself a glass of milk. As he watched Laura pile the freshly baked cookies onto a platter, he asked, "Feel like going to the lake today? We could work on the boat."

"You have to go to Springfield and I have to watch Tommy. My mother's out and my dad's gone golfing."

Don shook his head in disgust but he didn't say anything. Laura knew he was thinking her parents were irresponsible. Secretly, she was sort of glad that Don seemed to be more willing to see her side of things.

Tommy left the room for a few minutes and Don said, "I wanted to tell you that I thought a lot last night. One of the things I thought was that I've been too hard on you. I know you think that I take Gloria's side a lot. Last night, I decided that in a way, you're right. I guess I've just got to understand how you feel about her. The truth is . . . you seem so much more grown-up than Gloria in so many ways . . . I take her side because she's . . . maybe the word is frail."

"Gloria is *not* frail," Laura said crossly. "Gloria can hold her own and it isn't fair the way everyone always assumes she has to be protected. After all, she's an adult."

Don nodded. "I guess you're right. She's *your* mother. I could see that for the first time last night. Before that . . . I don't know . . . you'd always seemed so much in control . . . it was only after you'd done . . . only after I *thought* you'd done something childish . . . like run away. I think I understand, Laurie. You're only sixteen."

Laura laughed at him. "Don, you sound like you're thirty. Isn't it funny the way we both seem so much more grown-up than most adults? Maybe that's the secret attraction."

Tommy came back then and began demanding Laura's undivided attention. She looked at Don helplessly and said, "I hope you'll excuse us. It's Chinese checkers time."

Don stood up to go. He asked, "What time shall I pick you up this evening?"

A slight frown crossed Laura's face. "Oh, Don, I don't know. I have a feeling . . . the truth is . . . my folks had a fight. I don't know what's going to be happening tonight but I think I'd better be here. I hope you understand."

Whatever Don's emotions, he kept them to himself. He said, "Laurie, "I'll be home by six. If your plans change, call me. I'll be waiting for you."

Even though Tommy was in the room, she kissed Don good-bye and said, "I'll call you tonight or see you on the corner tomorrow morning."

If Tommy thought there was anything special about Laura kissing Don, he didn't say so. He seemed happy enough to play Chinese checkers and eat cookies until about four o'clock when he began asking again, "Is Mama ever going to come home?"

Laura hugged him swiftly and said, "Don't worry, Tommy. We'll be all right. Now what shall I cook for dinner?"

Tommy looked as though he might cry as he said, "Today is Sunday. How can Mama be shopping? Where is she?"

Laura didn't feel it was her place to tell Tommy lies. She said, "To tell you the truth, I'm not sure where Gloria is. But wherever she is, I'm sure she's having fun. So why don't we do the same? Would you be interested in helping me make chop suey? Daddy loves it."

"Chop suey comes from restaurants," Tommy complained. "I wish Mama would come home, don't you?"

Laura answered, "Right now I'm just glad to be home with you and Daddy. What I'm really think-ign about is how long it would take to make some sweet and sour spare ribs to go with the chop suey. We have some ribs in the freezer."

Laura tied an apron hanging on the kitchen hook around her Levis and went to the freezer to begin digging through the packaged meats for ribs. Tommy grumbled, "That's Mama's apron."

"You can wear mine," Laura offered from the depths of the freezer compartment.

Tommy was still grumbling to himself when Laura straightened up, holding a box of frozen snow peas in one hand and a package of meat in the other. She pronounced proudly, "Here are the beginnings of the most beautiful Chinese meal ever to be produced outside of Upper Mongolia."

The happier Tommy got as he chopped vegetables and sliced bits of leftover chicken, the more worried Laura became. She watched the clock anxiously, waiting for Gloria to walk in the door. Laura knew there was an A.A. meeting Sunday afternoon at three. Around four-thirty, she thought she heard Gloria several times.

When it got to be five and Gloria wasn't home, Laura decided she wouldn't be coming home. She didn't want to think about that, but there was a certain triumph in the way she managed to get

Tommy's attention off his mother and onto the dinner they were preparing. *He won't miss her long*, Laura thought. The minute she thought that, she felt guilty and deliberately turned her attention to the meal.

Tommy followed Laura around the kitchen, read to her from the cookbook, gave directions, and supervised every onion she sliced.

When her father came in, he asked in a soft voice, "Your mother?"

"She called about noon. When she found out I was home, she hung up." Laura felt sort of sick in the pit of her stomach as she answered her father. She was telling the literal truth but she knew she was slanting the facts.

"She all right?" He looked gray and worried in spite of his day in the sunshine.

"Dad, there was music in the background." For the first time, Laura acknowledged the unspoken worry. "I don't think she'd been drinking but I'm not sure. Her voice wasn't slurred."

John Manning shook his head heavily. "She should be home."

Laura added as nonchalantly as she could, "I told her you'd gone golfing."

He looked very upset by that news and Laura thought he might bawl her out, but all he said was, "I suppose she said I was irresponsible."

"Pots don't call kettles black," Laura said sharply.

John Manning patted Laura absently on the head and said, "Keep Tommy entertained. I'm going to make some calls."

"Don't start, please," Laura begged.

"Why not?"

Laura's face twisted and she bit her lip as the old memories flooded her mind. She said, "I can't bear the thought of you calling bar after bar, looking for your wayward wife. It was so humiliating. I hated it."

Her father looked at Laura in amazement. He said carefully, slowly, "You were young. You didn't understand. Your mother was a sick woman and I was sick with jealousy. No matter what you think, Gloria didn't spend a lot of time in bars. I often accused her of things that didn't happen. Don't make your mother the stock villain in this piece, Laura. It isn't fair, you know."

Before she could answer, he walked out of the kitchen. What was worse was that he didn't look back when she called out, "Wait until you see what we've prepared for dinner. It's a special surprise."

CHAPTER 17

As she put the finishing touches on dinner, Laura listened anxiously for the sound of the door opening. She was certain that Gloria would be home at dinnertime if she was coming home. Laura carried the steaming dishes to the table thinking, *Poor Daddy. First his daughter and then his wife run away. All in twenty-four hours. He's got a lot to put up with.*

She walked softly into the den where John Manning sat next to the telephone, staring at the wall. His soft brown hair hung over his forehead and his blue eyes were clouded with sorrow. Laura could tell from the expression on his face that he'd found out nothing. As she watched him, she felt as tender and protective toward him as she often did toward Tommy.

She also felt a thrill of pleasure as she remembered what he'd said to Gloria before she left. "If anything happens to Laura, I'll never forgive you." It was worth a lot to have heard those words. Laura spoke softly as she said, "Daddy, it's time to eat. We've waited an hour."

Her father looked up at her, his reverie broken.

He spoke harshly as he said, "Take her apron off. How dare you wear her apron!"

Startled by his sudden attack, Laura turned and walked from the room, untying the apron strings as she moved. She hung the apron on the kitchen hook, telling herself as she forced back the tears, *I've got to make allowances for him. Naturally he's upset. He's worried about Gloria.*

But try as she might, she couldn't make John Manning's attack on her all Gloria's fault. For one thing, her mother never tried to put the blame on other people. Her mother was always trying to make amends and take all the blame on herself. For another, it had been a long time since her father had really seemed to appreciate all that Laura did for him.

Nevertheless, Laura kept a cheerful face as she sat down at the table. She said, "Tommy and I worked and worked on this dinner. We call it the Manning Miracle Meal. Hope you like it."

Her father only took one spoonful of chop suey onto his plate and another spoonful of rice. Both children watched anxiously as he tasted it. He asked, "What is it?"

"Chop suey," Tommy said in a disgusted voice. It wasn't possible to tell whether he was disgusted with the food or his father.

Her father took another bite, then drank some of his tea. He said, "I'd rather have coffee."

Laura didn't argue. She got up from the table and made her father a cup of instant coffee. When she came back, she asked, "Aren't you going to try the sweet and sour ribs? They're made with a secret ingredient."

Laura winked at Tommy who giggled. It was he who had suggested adding the horse radish when they discovered they had no hot sauce or chili peppers.

At the sound of Tommy's small laugh, John Manning threw his napkin on the table and shouted at Laura, "You hope she never comes back, don't you? You hope she's out drinking somewhere. Ever since she got here, you've been hoping she'd get drunk."

Laura's face turned white as the blood drained from her face. What was happening to her father? It was the third time in twenty-four hours that he'd attacked her unreasonably. Didn't he see that he wasn't being fair? Didn't he understand that all she wanted was for them all to be happy again?

She spoke slowly, carefully, as though she were speaking to Tommy. At the same time, she tried to muster all her courage to defend herself. She could no longer trust John Manning. She didn't know what he might say next. "Daddy, I want us to be happy again. I want Tommy to stop crying all the time. I want you to stop yelling. Can't you see that ever since Gloria came here, there's been trouble?"

Tommy, who had been sitting white-faced, listening to the argument, started wailing at the sound of his name. Laura started toward him as John Manning said, "Came here? What do you mean — came *here*. Your mother came *home* and you're trying to drive her out. If she doesn't come back, I'll never forgive you."

Laura stared at her father's retreating back as John Manning left his home for the second time in one day. She was in a daze, but she was beginning to put things together in a slightly different way. *He's blaming it all on me now*, she thought. Earlier this morning, she had heard him use those exact words to his wife.

It's almost funny, she decided. The words "I'll never forgive you" had been wonderful at five in the morning and a curse at eight in the evening. Laura laughed softly, bitterly, as she began carrying the dishes in to the sink.

Tommy, who had been crying with varying intensity during the whole scene, asked, "Why was Daddy mad at you?"

"He's worried about Gloria."

"I'm worried about Gloria too," Tommy wailed. He crumpled into a ball and began kicking the table legs and pounding his fist on the table top for emphasis.

Laura watched Tommy dispassionately as she carried one plate after the other to the sink. She just didn't feel like trying to smooth things over and distract Tommy. He felt awful. Well, she felt awful too and she was sick of worrying about other people.

When she didn't react in the usual manner, Tommy opened one of his eyes and peeked at her while he wailed. She ignored him and he stopped kicking and pounding. He was still sniffling when he asked, "When is Mama coming home?"

"I don't know," Laura said dully. Though she knew Tommy was frightened, she was frightened too. It was as if the whole world had come apart and now she didn't know where to begin to pick up the pieces. She was beginning to see some things very differently than she ever had before.

One thing she saw clearly was the way her brother was behaving. *If he were someone else's brother, I'd say he's a brat*, she thought.

No wonder Don often seemed impatient when she couldn't do something because she had to help Tommy. Don also thought her father was spoiled. Laura sat down at the table and drank a cup of cold tea as she went over the events of yesterday and today. It was true her world was shattered to pieces, but she had an idea that she could put it together a little bit at a time. One thing she had to be sure about, she had to pick up the right pieces this time.

She said, "Tommy, go watch television. I want to think."

"But I'm *crying*," Tommy answered. His voice betrayed a mixture of bewilderment and demand, but Laura could hear no real pain.

Exactly how much of Tommy's fear is really a way to get attention? Laura asked herself. With effort, she forced herself to see her little brother in a realistic light. It was as if a newer, more grown-up part of herself became the observer.

Laura the Observer said cooly, *Tommy's spoiled. You've been so busy making it up to him, he's been getting away with murder*. Laura poured herself some more cold tea and said to her brother, "Go watch television. I'm thinking."

Tommy must have understood that she meant what she said. He stood up and started for the living room, but he paused long enough to accuse, "You *do* want Mama to drink. You're mean, Laurie. You're real mean."

Laura ignored Tommy because she was busy

asking herself the same question. It was clear that if she'd been so wrong about Tommy and about her father, she might be wrong about Gloria too. *Do I want her to drink?*

Laura put her elbows on the table and stared at the tea leaves in the bottom of the cup. She tried to let her mind go blank so that she could have the solitude she needed to look the situation over. Sometimes, when she had run a long, long way, Laura felt a certain kind of peace and pain mixture that she was feeling right now. She knew all she had to do was wait and she would find the right answer to her questions.

Laura sat for a long time in that thoughtful position. It was as if the Childish Laura was sitting still while Laura the Observer looked over the whole situation. *It's complicated*, Laura told herself. *Very complicated.* She felt as though she was moving around a lot of old pieces of her world, making them into new combinations. *Building a new way of looking at things*, Laura thought.

She saw things about herself that made her feel very good. It was true — she was special and she had tried very hard to do the right thing. *Too hard*, she reminded herself. It was clear that whatever else happened, she'd have to start letting Tommy and her father do more of the work, take more of the responsibility for their own actions.

Whatever mistakes she'd made, they'd been honest. She loved Tommy and her father very much and she'd done the best she could to fill in for her mother. *Yes, I did well*, Laura the Observer congratulated herself.

Even Don came under observation. Good, solid

Don had been exactly the sort of boyfriend needed, Laura the Observer decided. The old Laura was frightened of life and Don was frightened too. *I can help him*, Laura promised herself. *I can show him the way.* Yes, Don was solid and good and reliable. He was still wonderful, but he wasn't necessary in quite the same way. There would have to be some changes in that relationship too.

About that time, Tommy brought Laura a cup of instant coffee and said wistfully, "It's better than cold tea."

She thanked him for the coffee but did not discontinue her examination of herself and her world. When Tommy went quietly back to the living room without demanding attention, Laura thought, *He's already getting the message*. That would be the easiest mess to straighten out.

Her father would be a bit tougher. By this time, Laura the Observer had seen clearly that John Manning, troubled and burdened as he might be, was awfully good at escaping when things got tough. *He's isn't going to like having to behave like a parent*, Laura thought. She wasn't exactly sure how she was going to handle that one but she promised herself that she would really try.

That leaves Gloria, she reminded herself. Laura sighed as she drank the instant coffee. Anyone could see that she'd been pretty miserable on that count. No wonder Don always took Gloria's part. Aloud, she admitted, "I *did* want her to drink."

As soon as the words were out of her mouth, Laura felt better. It was true and everyone else knew it before she did. From the very beginning, she'd resented her mother's return. Though she'd made a pretense at cooperating most of the time, she hadn't given an extra inch.

I did want her to drink, but I don't now, Laura thought. She looked anxiously at the clock on the wall. It was almost ten. Past time to put Tommy to bed. Past time to finish the dishes. She took a deep breath and stood up. Her thinking was done. Her work was cut out for her.

First things first, Laura reminded herself, then she laughed aloud. That was one of her mother's Alcoholics Anonymous slogans. Well, it was true. So was the one that said, "Live twenty-four hours at a time."

She'd clean things up and put Tommy to bed. Her mother would come in eventually. She might be drunk. She might be sober, but Gloria would be back even if Laura had to go out and beg her to return. *After all,* she thought, *I may have been resentful and jealous, but she's my mother and I love her.*

CHAPTER 18

Gloria and John Manning came in together at
eleven o'clock. Gloria said, "Hi, Laura. Sorry
about sticking you with the dinner and dishes but
I went to two A.A. meetings."

"I dragged her out of the second one," her
father announced. "We had a long talk."

Laura's first reaction was cold fury. How dare
they look so happy! Her second reaction was
relief that her mother was sober. She wasn't sure
which feeling was the one that made her burst into
tears.

Her parents didn't try to touch her, but they
urged her to sit down in the wing chair in the
living room. Between sobs, Laura said wryly,
"This seems to be getting to be a habit."

When she'd finished the worst of the crying, her
father said, "Laurie, Baby . . ."

"Don't call her baby," Gloria warned sharply.

Laura could tell they'd rehearsed this speech
too. Well, this time she was prepared. This time
she had a speech of her own ready. She waited
quietly while her father began.

"Laura, I want to apologize. I realize — your mother has made me realize — that I'm quick to put the blame on anyone but myself."

He seemed to be waiting for Laura to contradict this, but she smiled and waited for him to continue.

"In fact, your mother feels . . . that is, we feel . . . you've been sorely tried by the demands that Tommy and I placed on you these last two years. Your mother feels that you're not only angry at her, but at me." John Manning smiled tentatively and waited for Laura's reassurance.

Laura looked at Gloria in amazement. *I was right*, Laura thought. *Gloria is not only tougher than they thought but smarter than I thought.*

"I think Gloria is right. I think you never even realized how much you expected of me. I'm only sixteen. I was only fourteen when Gloria left."

John Manning looked as though he might cry. He gulped and continued. "Your mother says you're actually healthier since she came home. She points out that your ulcer is gone and you are able to show your emotions easier."

Laura opened her mouth to object but then she closed it. Maybe it was at least partly true. Certainly, she hadn't taken a pill in weeks.

John Manning cleared his throat. What was coming next was clearly difficult for him. "We've decided to offer you a chance to escape us. You once counted on going to Miss Merriweather's School. You had a scholarship and you were cheated of that chance. Now, we're going to find the money for you to go for your last year of high school. Your mother will get a job and I'll cut out golf." He looked like Tommy when he was caught stealing cookies. "I should have used that golf money for a housekeeper a long time ago."

Laura was tempted by the offer. How had her mother known how much she'd wanted to go to Miss Merriweather's? She looked gratefully at her parents and said, "Thank you, but no thank you. I'm going to be a senior and you'll need me at home. Gloria has to go to meetings." She turned to her father and said with a slight tease in her voice, "But you can still cut down on your golf. I'll need help at the University of Massachusetts the year after this."

Gloria laughed aloud at the obvious discomfort of her husband. Then she said solemnly, "I know you're angry with me, Laura. You have every right to be. Not just for the past but for the present. My moodiness and childish behavior hasn't been easy."

"You're not drunk," Laura said. "I was afraid you'd be drinking."

Gloria shook her head and said, "I was just about to promise you a better future, but all I can really guarantee is to try."

"I want to apologize," Laura said abruptly. She had to get the words out. "I want to tell you that it's true — I did want you to drink. But I don't want you to drink now. I want you to get well. I love you."

When Gloria finished wiping her eyes, Laura went on. "I did a lot of thinking and I have some things to say. Most of them can wait, but Tommy is important. I think I've spoiled Tommy rotten.

Will you help me? I want you to promise not to do even more of it. We've got to sit down and make up a list of rules, and then we've got to follow them. Can you do it?"

Gloria took a deep, tremulous breath and said, "I'll try. Yes, I can do it."

"Good. I'm going to stop trying so hard." She grinned at her parents. "Actually, it's up to you two to finish the job."

She stood up, stretched, and said, "Tomorrow is the last week of school. I'm going to spend this summer learning to be a teenager. I'm going to the lake, to the movies, and I think I'll start reading romantic novels."

She kissed John and Gloria Manning goodnight and said wryly, "Don't try to make time stand still. I want to see Don tomorrow morning so don't turn off my alarm, please."

Her parents looked shocked at the suggestion that they might do such a thing. Laura didn't argue or remind them of the past. She'd done enough work for one night.